Cover by Pictor

Printed and published in Great Britain by D. C. Thomson & Co., Ltd., 185 Fleet Stret, London EC4A 2HS
© D. C. Thomson & Co., Ltd., 1991. While every reasonable care will be taken, neither D. C. Thomson &
Co., Ltd., nor its agents will accept liability for loss or damage to colour transparencies or any other
material submitted to this publication.

Magic In The Air

How do you change a lifelong pal into a sweetheart? Well, when all else fails, just close your eyes and make a wish . . .

Complete Story By **D. L. GARRARD**

THE first time Dan Mallory laid eyes on his daughter Sandra's new teddy-bear, he burst out laughing.

"Did you ever see such a cynical expression on a bear's face?" he exclaimed. "He must be a direct descendant of Diogenes!"

Sandra, only two years old and not knowing as much about Greek philosophers as her schoolteacher father, didn't know why he laughed, but liked the name all the same.

"Dodgy Knees!" she said gleefully, and the name stuck.

In fact, she was happy with Dodgy Knees for six whole years — until the day she suddenly announced to the boy next door that she wanted a kitten.

"Why?" George Granger asked.

The two children were perched like a couple of birds in the branches of the ancient apple tree that spread over both sides of the fence dividing the Grangers' garden from the Mallorys'.

"Because Dodgy Knees doesn't listen any more."

"Ah," George said wisely. He understood how Sandra felt. His more dignified Edward Bear had been laid to rest some years back, when a similar lack of communication had become apparent.

He shifted on his branch. He was ten years old, he reminded himself, two years older than Sandra. Too old to be her friend, really, but he'd known her all her life, after all. Anyway, she made him laugh, she was so mischievous.

On top of that, she was only small, and needed protecting. It made him feel good, taking care of her whenever he could . . .

So while he didn't mention her at all to his mates at school, he continued to meet Sandra up the apple tree on Saturday mornings — escaping the boring weekly shopping expedition with his mother.

Now he looked at Sandra thoughtfully. "I thought girls played with dolls and things until they were quite old," he said. "Till they got babies to play with instead?"

"That's too long to wait," she replied. "I want something that will really listen to me — something with *alive ears!*"

"Dogs' ears are nice," George said.

"Dogs are too noisy. I wish I had a kitten."

The kitten didn't land in her lap, exactly.

But a moment later, it came slithering down from a high branch, where it had been crouching, petrified, for goodness knows how long. A small ball of black fur with needle claws, quivering whiskers and huge, astonished green eyes.

Sandra reached out and lifted it gently from the branch.

"That's magic," she whispered in an awed voice.

George, too, was amazed, but he tried not to show it. "Somebody'll claim it," he said practically. "A dog must have chased it up there or something. You'll have to put a notice on your gate — or a card in the sweet-shop window."

"Have I got to?" Sandra asked, her face stricken.

"Well, Sandy, it isn't yours, is it?" George pointed out.

"P'raps this is a wishing tree," Sandra said hopefully.

"It's a Beaconsfield apple tree, Dad said."

"But it's so old it doesn't have apples any more. Maybe it's changed into something else. P'raps it'll grant me three wishes like in fairy stories!" She closed her eyes tight. "I wish this kitten was mine!" she cried.

"You've already wished for a kitten — now you've wished for this one." George shook his head. "Two wishes and one to go. Wasteful!" he observed with calm logic.

But Sandra, with the kitten in her arms, was oblivious. And her happiness increased as a whole month went by and no-one came to claim the kitten.

"You see," Sandra said to George. "It *is* a wishing tree. Fluffpuss is mine."

"*Fluffpuss!*" George groaned. But the months passed and the name stuck.

EVENTUALLY Sandra and George stopped climbing the tree, but they still chatted over the fence, with a fat Fluffpuss incredibly balanced on the top of it.

Sandra needed a maths consultant for homework, and George enjoyed a sample of whatever Sandra had brought home from cookery class. She'd always been better at the practical subjects. When it came to maths she just seemed to go round and round in circles.

"I'll never pass my 'O'-levels," she moaned, as the exams loomed ominously near. "I wish . . ."

"Careful!" George said solemnly. "That's the third wish. Don't waste it."

He was 18 now and assured of a place at university. His ginger hair had changed to a wavy fairness, and his features had taken on a rugged handsomeness.

"I don't think it would be a waste," Sandra argued. "My parents will be really disappointed if I don't make it to teachers' training college."

"But if you need a wish to get through 'O'-levels you'll never manage the 'A's without, will you? Save it for then,"

"You may be right," Sandra agreed after a moment.

"Anyway, you'll make it without wishes," George assured her. "You can do anything, if you try hard enough."

"I don't think you want me to use that third wish," Sandra reflected. "You've always found some reason to stop me using it, ever since Fluffpuss arrived. You're always telling me there's something I'll want more one day."

UNCANNY!

While visiting friends, I could hardly believe my eyes. I saw their neighbour go out into her garden carrying a tray with an assortment of tins upon it, and stop at a cupboard lying on the path.

Curiously, I watched as she carefully placed the tray on the lawn. She then proceeded to open all the tins with a can opener fastened to the cupboard. Bemused, I just couldn't resist asking her what she was doing.

The explanation? The previous evening her husband had taken down the cupboard from her kitchen and put up a new one . . . but he forgot to remove their one and only can opener from the old cupboard he'd thrown out!

A CANINE

by MARY KEMP

AFTER a hard day's work rounding up the cattle, Shep, the black and white sheepdog, likes to take the weight off his paws by going for a brisk horse ride.

Mandy, the Welsh mountain pony, waits patiently in her stable for Shep to finish work. Then Shep is hoisted on to Mandy's back by their owner, 21-year-old Bethan Lloyd, and hangs on doggedly(!) as Mandy trots over the nearby fields.

Shep was just a pup when he learned to ride six years ago. Since then, he has progressed in leaps and bounds, even taking the odd jump or two.

Farmer's daughter Bethan told me, "It all started as a bit of a joke. One day, after I'd been out riding, I put Shep on Mandy's back to see if he liked it. He took to it straightaway although, at that time, Mandy was just standing still.

"Then Shep began following me on foot when I went out on Mandy. There is a busy road at the top of our drive and, because I was frightened that Shep would run across and get knocked down by a car, I made him sit behind me."

Motorists could hardly believe their eyes when they saw Shep happily riding the pony. As Bethan said, "They were too surprised to say anything. They just pointed and stared."

Now Bethan is taking Shep over some jumps on Mandy, but the lessons are proving painful.

"Shep isn't getting on very well," explained Bethan. "He keeps falling off all the time. I think he needs a bit more practice.

"Mandy really enjoys taking Shep for a ride on the flat, though. I've had her since I was seven years old and, like Shep, I learned to ride on her. She's so good natured and gentle.

"But Mandy is an old lady now and I'm too big to ride her. So she's all Shep's!"

MANDY has taught Shep that it's a lot easier to ride than to run. So he hitches lifts on the farm tractors or even a wheelbarrow.

Beth, a groom from Manorwen in Pembrokeshire, Wales, added, "Even when I carry a bale of straw across the yard, Shep will jump on to it."

"And so you might. You got your bike without a wish. Your mother let you go abroad on that school trip. And so on . . ."

"Well, if there's no more of that Scotch Egg, I'd better be off. Got a date with Juliana tonight."

"You and all your girlfriends!" Sandra shook her head helplessly. "Why is it you always pick ones with fancy names?"

But George only grinned.

That August George went north to stay with relatives, before going straight on to university. Sandra went to a holiday camp with friends. She wrote him a postcard.

Mum sent on my exam results today. Pretty measly. Decided not to stay on at school, I'm going to start work in the local bank. There's a Phyllida in Chalet 15, but she's not interested in boys with ordinary names.

HITCH-HIKER!

But when there is work to be done around the farm, Shep is always in the running. His chores include fetching the Lloyds' herd of 65 dairy cows for milking, and putting a gaggle of geese to bed at night.

Bethan explained, "If Shep hasn't got work to do, he goes missing. But we always know he will be in the field playing with Mandy. She chases him, he chases her — they're up and down the whole time.

"In fact, they're absolutely devoted to one another. Shep should really sleep in the shed where we keep the calves, because he's a farm dog. But, if he gets the chance, he's in Mandy's stable like a shot."

But, when Shep becomes too much of a burden, he is usually riding for a fall. One quick shake is all it takes for Mandy to get rid of that doggone rider. ■

George wrote back after he had settled in at university.

Dear Sandy,

Bad luck. But with sex equality you could get to be a bank manager and handle my overdraft sympathetically. Sharing a pad here with a fellow called Rod Barker. Have found a Kirsten, an Evadne and a Genevieve already. Life's great, but I'm missing my Supplementary Benefits from cookery class. What's happening to the left-overs now?

A T Christmas, George brought Rod home for the festive season. Sandra went round to the Grangers' with George's present and was confronted by a tall dark stranger with melting brown eyes. Rod also had an endearing clumsiness which brought a worried look into Mrs Granger's eyes whenever he was near anything breakable.

But when he smiled at Sandra her heart banged suddenly against her ribs, and she just couldn't look away . . .

She stayed on, listening to Rod's slow, lazy voice telling her about life at university. George, naturally, had girls to see, now he was home.

"We'll have to find someone for you, Rod," he said, getting ready to go out.

Sandra held her breath as Rod smiled at her. "Why not Sandra?"

"Sandra?" George gave her a startled look.

"Well . . . er . . ."

"I think we'll get on fine," Rod said. "How about it, Sandra?"

"Thank you. I'd love to." And the look she gave George should have slain him on the spot.

The Christmas holidays were short, but long enough for Sandra to feel herself growing more and more miserable as the day of Rod's departure approached.

"You must write to me," he told her, taking her hand at the railway station, and smiling.

"Of course," she replied, trying to keep her voice light.

They gazed at each other, while George thumped his fists together. It had been snowing hard, and a fresh flurry powdered the hood of Sandra's coat.

"Train's late," George grumbled. "And the loudspeaker system always seems to have laryngitis."

"I'll go and see if there's any news," Rod said.

He moved away up the platform to check with a porter. George was looking at Sandra with a frown.

"Pity your father couldn't drive you back," she said brightly. "But it wouldn't be safe with the roads as they are."

"Sandy . . ." George began, but couldn't seem to get anything else out except clouds of steam in the bitter cold air.

Rod came galloping back. "It's been delayed — but there's a relief train on platform two. It's going any minute."

They hurried over the bridge with cases and holdalls. The train thrummed impatiently as George hauled his luggage inside. Rod dropped a light kiss on Sandra's forehead.

"I'll see you again, Sweet Sixteen," he said softly.

A T Easter, George visited Rod's parents. During the summer vacation, he returned alone. Sandra asked him why Rod hadn't come with him.

"Rod?" he said in surprise at Sandra's over-casual enquiry. "He's gone on holiday with his parents. Then he's going somewhere or other with friends."

"You didn't tell me . . . "

"But he writes to you, doesn't he?"

"Now and then," Sandra answered vaguely.

"Look, Sandy, can't you find yourself a local boyfriend?" George

suggested. "Somebody nearer your age?"

"I could if I wanted to," she assured him stiffly. "I just happen to prefer Rod, that's all."

George looked concerned. "Look, Rod's . . . Well, *look*, Sandy . . . that 'mother-me' air about him — he uses it all the time. The girls fall for him like ninepins."

"Really," Sandra said coldly. "What with the Bernices and the Alexandras swooning around you, as well, your room must be absolutely littered!"

Then she stalked away — and shed a few tears in private.

A T Christmas George brought Rod again. But this time it was different.

For that evening, George, dancing with his current girlfriend, Sylvia, looked over at Sandra and blinked. And, in that moment, he realised Sandy, the funny adolescent, had gone. In her place was a very lovely young lady — with eyes only for Rod.

"Are you dancing with me, or your young friend?" Sylvia inquired.

"Young is the operative word," he growled.

"Is Rod so dangerous?" Sylvia inquired with interest.

"It isn't that," George said irritably.

"Then what is it?" Sylvia persisted.

11

"She's no experience of people like Rod. He's a great guy — a good mate — but he'll never get emotionally involved until he's done his round-the-world bit, and got established in his profession. He's a loner, and he's broken more hearts than — than —"

"Than you have?" Sylvia murmured dryly. "You should talk! We girls have to learn the hard way — by experience. Stop clucking, George, you're like a hen with a wayward chick."

"But I feel sort of responsible," George muttered.

Sylvia laughed. "Some responsibility! I'll bet she's been turning heads since kindergarten!"

"What? Last year she was a cross between Minnie Mouse and — and Bugs Bunny!"

Sylvia's eyebrows rose disbelievingly. "All right — so she blossomed overnight. But watch it, George, you'll embarrass the girl if you don't stop acting like a parent!"

After the holidays were over, Sandra's letters to Rod took on a new depth. They were warm, leisurely, full of personal thoughts — almost like diaries. The pattern of her daily life; the endearing and comical habits of Fluffpuss; the colour of the sky at daybreak when she couldn't sleep for thinking about him; the rain after dark making diamonds on the window pane and whispering his name . . .

George, shamefully, read a page or two. Then, fascinated, read a few more. How could he help it, he asked himself crossly, when Rod left them openly littered all over the room for anyone to see!

He knew Rod left most of the letters unanswered, so he started writing more letters to Sandra himself. Somehow, he just couldn't lose his feeling of responsibility — and it got worse when Rod cleared a pile of her letters into the waste-paper basket.

Finally, he decided not to ask Rod home again, but that didn't make him feel any better. After all, if Rod wanted to see her, he'd travel down anyway . . .

Bemused, he took to gnawing his knuckles and kept getting his girls' names mixed up, which didn't make his own life exactly simple.

Then Sandra came up to attend graduation with his parents, looking chic in a green linen and very lovely suit.

"Guess what, George?" she said. "You know I'm eighteen next month — well, our parents have decided to give us a joint birthday and graduation party. Last March, a gale blew down the old fence, so we're spreading it right across the two gardens. Chinese lanterns on the wishing tree and floodlights on the fish pond!"

Then, her blue eyes shining, she turned and looked at Rod. "You'll come, won't you? It's a double-invitation, so you can't refuse!" She smiled.

"How could I refuse?" Rod responded lazily. "So long as it happens before I set off for Morocco."

"Morocco?" Sandra looked puzzled.

"I've a cousin working there. As good a place as any to aim for, for the first leg of my trip," he explained. "Excuse me for a moment — someone wants me. See you later, Seventeen."

"What trip?" Sandra asked George, when Rod had gone.

Continued on page 14

BY
CAROL
GOW

AN extremely short-sighted friend of mine once remarked that not being able to see too clearly made life more interesting. She continues to gaze mistily ahead and goes her merry way boarding wrong buses and greeting complete strangers as long lost friends.

But, unlike my friend, who takes life as it comes, I prefer to know exactly which bus I'm boarding and where it will take me.

It took a couple of incidents to prove finally to me that my vision is not exactly one hundred per cent., or even forty-nine per cent. come to that.

Out with a new boyfriend, I urged him to run for a bus as we didn't want to be late for the concert we were going to.

Looking at me rather strangely, he did as I suggested and we reached the bus stop breathless but much warmer.

After a good deal of confusion he finally pointed out that what I'd mistaken for a green corporation bus was, in fact, a woman coming down the road sporting a corporation-green beret.

The final proof that something had to be done came when I hopped into a car which pulled up alongside me, thinking how nice it was of Mike to stop and give me a lift to work.

I hopped out again pretty smartish, giving the astonished man a garbled apology about mistaking the car, and collided with his very aggressive looking wife, who was wearing a red mac and a suspicious face.

On some devilish impulse, I blew him a kiss and ran off leaving him to his fate.

However, after that I decided that Something Would Have To Be Done. But what? I hated the idea of wearing glasses. Why not contact lenses?

The eye s have it

**Until I discovered contact lenses
life had all the clarity of
an optical illusion!**

The optician, when I finally tracked him down, was very encouraging, and at my next appointment he suggested a trial run. He popped two minute lenses into my eyes and sent me out for an hour to see how my eyes would react.

"Just walk about for a while, and avoid centrally-heated shops," he suggested helpfully. "And keep your eyes down, there will be less irritation that way," he added, propelling me to the door.

With great timing about ten yards from the shop, I ran into a very old friend who'd just come home from Australia.

I shudder to think what she thought of my enthusiastic welcome.

I stared at my feet the whole time and blew my nose noisily, tears trickling down my chin. "Bust dash," I mumbled through wads of paper tissues. "I've got ad appoitbed — I'll telephode you toborrow."

A couple of centuries later I got back to my optician's.

"Very satisfactory," he concluded and within a week, he issued me with my very own little case complete with lenses and sundry bottles of solution.

Everything's fine on the eye front now, but, if you ever see someone groping around the pavement blindly, fingers probing every square dusty inch, do stop and give me a hand. They're very tiny, contact lenses, and so expensive to replace . . . ∎

Continued from page 12

"His Round-The-World-In-Two-Years Trip," George replied brusquely. "Come on, the parents are waiting to take photographs and I want to get out of this gown before somebody spills strawberries and cream on it."

It was a good thing Sandra wasn't taking the pictures, he thought morosely — her hands were trembling so much she couldn't have held the camera.

SANDRA made sure that the party happened before Morocco. The double garden looked quite vast in the summer dusk. White moths fluttered round the lanterns on the wishing tree, fairy lights draped the outer fences. There was music, food and drink, and all the makings of a memorable night.

Sandra looked enchanting in a flame-coloured dress, and Rod was obviously impressed. She took him to the wishing tree and leaned back against the bark. He stood over her, one hand resting on a branch above her head.

"When are you going to Morocco?" Sandra asked.

"Next week," Rod replied.

"When will you be back?"

"This year, next year, sometime, never — who knows."

"I wish," Sandra said, and her fingers pressed the bark of the tree so that her knuckles grew white, "I wish you'd take me with you."

Rod grinned. "No go, sorry, Seventeen."

"Eighteen," Sandra said.

"Of course. Eighteen. Remember the saying — He who travels alone travels fastest."

"Do you have to travel fastest?"

"Not necessarily. But alone, yes. Just me and a sleeping bag — and freedom."

She stared up at him.

His lazy, soothing voice, his beguiling expression, still masked a stranger. She had never really known him. And now he was going and he wouldn't come back.

He bent and kissed her lightly then started to turn away. "Those are super Scotch Eggs you made," he said. "Better go and grab another before they all vanish."

Then, in a moment, he was gone.

Sandra groped her way to the dark side of the tree and stumbled over George. He was sitting alone, his knees were drawn up under his chin, and he nodded towards the buffet table.

"They're wasted on him," he said. "Rod wouldn't know Scotch Eggs from Irish Stew. Stomach like a vacuum cleaner."

Sandra didn't reply.

He stood up. "Sandy — I was here when you came over with Rod. I didn't want to show myself and embarrass you."

Still she said nothing. He tilted her chin upwards.

"Hey," he said softly. Then he bent his head and they touched foreheads briefly.

"George," she whispered, and huge tears brimmed and spilled. "Oh, George . . ."

"Sandy, I'm sorry."

"No — you warned me. And I knew really, anyway. What a fool I am," she choked. "A wishing tree — at my age!"

"It wasn't foolish at all. Two wishes brought you Fluffpuss. The third would have worked, only I beat you to it. You see, I stole it," George confessed in a quiet voice.

"Oh, George! Always trying to save my silly face!" She gave a sob that was half a laugh.

He pushed a handkerchief into her hands and put his arms round her.

"Have a good blow. Go on."

She blew obediently. "What did you need a wish for, anyway?"

"I didn't intend to pip you at the post," George said. "I was just sitting there, holding my breath and trying not to listen, and suddenly it all became clear to me. I said to myself 'Mirandas and Belladonnas are ten a penny, but really and truly there's only one Sandra. I wish she was mine'." He smiled at her expression.

"Well . . . eighteen years of borrowing my handkerchiefs and climbing my apple tree must have been leading up to something . . ."

A comforting, familiar warmth stole round Sandra's heart. "Time will tell," she said at last.

"Yes," George agreed masterfully. "But somehow, Sandy, I don't think there's much doubt about what it will say."

——————— * **THE END** * ———————

"Where Did Our Love Go?"

HERE in the sun on the small patio, I look at the roses that need pruning since Paul left, and wonder sadly what to do with Fudge's things.

I've got them here with me.

His collar, his lead, a bit chewed where he carried it around waiting for walks, his heavy dish and his battered plastic water bowl.

I've even got his coat — the red one Paul bought him — and I push it out of sight hurriedly. I don't want to think of Paul. But I can't help it . . .

Paul bought Fudge for me. We'd only been married for two years then, and our first baby, Jamie, had just been born. We'd left Jamie with my mother while we'd gone to buy a new set of saucepans. But, instead, we bought Fudge.

"Paul! Aren't those puppies absolutely gorgeous!" I said, catching

How could she ever find the answer — she, the wife who was too wrapped up in herself to even face up to the question . . . ?

Paul's hand in mine as we stared in the pet shop window.

I dragged him inside over to the basket of crawling, fluffy, floppy puppies. There were five of them, all different sorts and shapes, and one of them was huddled forlornly in the corner with bits of straw sticking to long curly ears.

"Oh, Paul!" I couldn't help the longing in my voice. We couldn't really afford a puppy, but I really wanted one. When I'd lived with my parents, we'd always had an assortment of animals at home — dogs, cats, rabbits, mice.

I hung over the puppies and Paul stood silently beside me. A little forlorn one blinked up at me with huge brown eyes, and put out a pink wet tongue hopefully.

"He's so sweet!" I said to the assistant standing beside the basket.

"Yes, and only five bob to you," he said cheerfully. "Keep you company when the old man's at work," he added, grinning widely at Paul, who hesitated.

"Paul?" I asked in a small voice.

He shrugged, then grinned, digging hard into his pocket.

"OK, Holly," he said. "But you'll have to feed him out of the housekeeping."

We were halfway home on the bus, the puppy a warm bundle

Complete Story By ELIZABETH ASHCROFT

against my chest, wrapped in my scarf, when I turned to Paul sitting beside me.

"What do you think it is?" I asked. "A bitch, or a dog?"

He smiled. "I don't know! Does it matter?"

"Of course!" I said indignantly. "It means we either call it Henry or Henrietta, for a start!"

In the end we called the little scrap Fudge. I'd been making some the day before and it was only when Paul stole a piece from the plate that I realised it was exactly the same colour as the puppy.

"That's what we'll call him!" I said delightedly. "Fudge!"

However, Mother was horrified. "A four-month-old baby and a puppy! What are you thinking of, Holly?"

"They'll grow up together," I told her. "And Jamie will love him when he grows older. Fudge can look after him in his pram in the garden."

B

Fudge did just that, too. He sat on guard over Jamie's pram, wuffling warningly as soon as anyone came up the path to the basement flat where we lived. Then, when Carol was born two years later, Fudge followed her around, puzzled as she crawled, tolerant as she walked, and gently rebuffing her when she pulled his ears or trod on his long swishy tail.

He was, we decided, part-spaniel, part-dachshund.

He had a long, low body, a spaniel's head with soulful eyes, and ears so long he frequently fell over them when he was in a hurry. He spent the first few months of his life in trouble — either for chewing Paul's shoes or hiding Jamie's toys when he threw them out of the pram.

Then we moved to Three Trees.

Paul had been promoted, the children were growing up, and the flat had been too small for us all.

We expanded gratefully at the new house. The children went to school just down the road, Paul began staying out all day for lunch instead of coming home, and I got myself a job.

I spent my mornings rushing round doing the housework, cooking the evening meal, and my afternoons in the Flower Pot selling exotic plants and packets of seeds. Paul thought I was doing too much.

"You look tired, Holly," he said once.

I flinched inwardly. That, to a woman, means she looks old.

"Do I?" I said, and next day made an appointment to have my hair cut and permed.

I went on a diet and bought new clothes. And afterwards, I surveyed myself in the mirror with a pleased smile. I didn't look like the mother of two children but Paul didn't even seem to notice the "New Me."

I was tired, even though I wouldn't admit it.

The meals still had to be cooked, the washing still had to be done and Fudge still had to be walked twice a day.

We had a routine by then. I took him out first thing, at nine o'clock, after everyone had disappeared in their various directions, and when I came home after work. I began to look forward to those walks with Fudge as the quiet moments in my life.

We would go down by the riverbank, and I'd throw twigs for him. He'd gallop off and forget what he'd been looking for, and begin nosing around in the long daisy-covered grass at half-forgotten scents. Once, he even fell in the river.

NOW I look down at his basket, chewed at one side, some of the cane missing, and remember that morning.

It was a Saturday, and for once Paul had been with me. The children must have been about nine and seven, for Mother had taken them off to the zoo together.

"It'll give you and Paul a chance to be alone for once," she'd said meaningfully, and for a moment I'd wondered why she should have said it.

★   ★   ★   ★

"Coming, Paul?" I asked, duffel coat round my shoulders, my trousers tucked inside wellington boots.

"Where to?" He was finishing breakfast in the dining-room, head in the newspaper and a cup of coffee half-finished by his side.

"Along the river with Fudge," I said brightly. "It's a gorgeous day."

And suddenly, achingly, I wanted him to come. We never seemed to go anywhere together. There just wasn't time.

He was either at a meeting, or I was working, or the kids were quarrelling or wanted help with projects from school. And suddenly I saw what Mother had meant.

We didn't spend much time together now. I looked at Paul and a thought flashed through my mind — I didn't know him any more. I didn't know what he thought or felt any more. We were almost strangers . . .

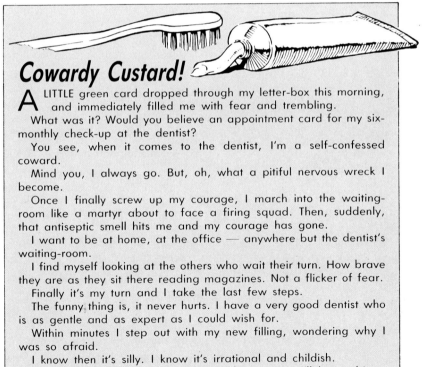

Cowardy Custard!

A LITTLE green card dropped through my letter-box this morning, and immediately filled me with fear and trembling.

What was it? Would you believe an appointment card for my six-monthly check-up at the dentist?

You see, when it comes to the dentist, I'm a self-confessed coward.

Mind you, I always go. But, oh, what a pitiful nervous wreck I become.

Once I finally screw up my courage, I march into the waiting-room like a martyr about to face a firing squad. Then, suddenly, that antiseptic smell hits me and my courage has gone.

I want to be at home, at the office — anywhere but the dentist's waiting-room.

I find myself looking at the others who wait their turn. How brave they are as they sit there reading magazines. Not a flicker of fear.

Finally it's my turn and I take the last few steps.

The funny thing is, it never hurts. I have a very good dentist who is as gentle and as expert as I could wish for.

Within minutes I step out with my new filling, wondering why I was so afraid.

I know then it's silly. I know it's irrational and childish.

I know something else. Next time I have to go I'll be as big a coward all over again!

"Come on, Paul," I said again hopefully, and he shrugged, getting up reluctantly.

"OK. Anything for a quiet life."

But as we walked through the sunny spring day I felt a chill run through me. He grudges half an hour with me, I thought bitterly.

And I remembered another day like this — with the sun bright on crocuses peeping out at the foot of the trees in the park . . .

I turned impulsively to Paul.

"Don't you remember?" I asked softly. "We bought Fudge on a day like this."

He looked down at me and there was something in his eyes that made me wonder. Almost a look of recognition, as though he, too, was remembering the way we once were.

"So it was," he said, "a long time ago." He watched as Fudge ran backwards and forwards among the long grass under the trees.

"He's getting old, Holly," he added, and suddenly my eyes misted.

I'd never thought about Fudge getting old. He was part of my life, seemed even to be part of my marriage.

"He's only about ten!" I said angrily, and ran after him, leaving Paul strolling along behind. I threw Fudge's ball for him and he made a dive for it, and slid with a protesting surprised yelp into the river.

"Fudge!" I screamed. "Fudge! Paul, he'll drown!"

"Don't be silly!" Paul ran and caught my arm as I tried to scramble down the bank after Fudge. "He can swim! All dogs can swim!"

"But he can't get up the bank!" I tore myself away and scrambled down towards Fudge, who swam to me gratefully, and, of course, I went in — up to my knees in squelching icy water.

I hauled Fudge up on to the bank, and looked into Paul's furious eyes.

"You idiot!" he exploded. "You'll catch pneumonia! He'd have been perfectly all right. Sometimes I think you care more for that dog than you do for me!"

"Paul . . ." I spluttered. "Don't be silly!"

Fudge raced round in circles, uttering shrill yips of joy, but I ignored him. My teeth chattered violently and I thought only that our wonderful spring walk was ruined — and that Paul was angry. He seemed to get angry so easily these days.

But half an hour later as I stood under the shower, I wondered why. After all, I did care for him, didn't I? Of course I did — why else did I go out to work, to buy new clothes to make me look smart when he took me out. My thoughts juddered to a stop.

When did he ever take me out, though?

We hadn't been out for months, the last time was to the firm's Christmas Dance. He never came home and unexpectedly announced that we were going out for dinner; never suggested an outing with the kids to the coast. Yet at one time we'd gone once a month to the sea, or the hills, picnicking . . .

A prickle of fear hit me. He'd changed. Had I changed, too?

I didn't think so.

I was a bit tired, true. I was angry with the kids occasionally, when they came in with mud on their shoes or made a muddle in the sitting-room when I'd just tidied it.

THE WRITING ON THE WALL

Do you ever have one of those "off" days, when you get out of bed on the wrong side and disaster follows upon disaster, until you feel like screaming . . . ?

Well, here's what I do when I feel that everything's getting on top of me.

First, I take a large, blank sheet of paper, and stick it up in a prominent position on the wall. Then, as soon as I begin to feel irritated or even blazing mad, I pick up the nearest pen and get to work on that paper. I write down all my grievances and troubles in bold, black letters. Although the result may be unprintable, I feel a great deal better for it afterwards.

Mind you, when I've calmed down a bit, I make sure I destroy the evidence, or I could find myself in a very embarrassing situation if my family saw what I'd said about them!

But surely everyone had their off-days now and again? I got dressed and went downstairs. The house was oddly quiet. Paul hadn't come home from the river. He'd looked unforgiving and melancholy, oddly lonely, his shoulders hunched as he'd disappeared round the tow path.

Fudge was sitting by the gas fire, and his thick tail thumped welcomingly on the rug. I'd dried him off and given him a biscuit to console him, and suddenly my eyes misted with tears.

Fudge was the only one who never changed, I thought. He was always there, always loving, no matter what happened. I sat there in my dressing-gown, struggling with tears. So much for Mother's idea of giving Paul and me a few hours together, I thought woefully. We'd finished up further apart than ever.

For a moment I thought of giving up my job. But we'd come to rely on the money, and without it I wouldn't know what to do with myself, anyway. The house was empty all day with the children at school and I'd be terribly lonely.

So we continued in the same way. And I tried to pretend we were just going through a phase. That we weren't really drifting apart . . .

THEN Paul had his accident. He was coming home from work when he'd swerved to avoid another car and had crashed. He broke his leg and was at home for weeks.

During that time we grew closer, walking with Fudge when Paul was able to swing along on crutches, and I finished decorating the kitchen, which Paul had begun the day before his accident.

Life was fun again, simply because we were together, doing all the same things together.

I phoned the shop and told them I couldn't work for a few weeks, and because they were busy they said they'd find someone else to take my place.

Secretly, I was relieved. But Paul was furious.

"You fool!" he raged. "Of all the times to pack up work."

I stared at him in astonishment. "But I wanted to be with you while you're at home!" I said heatedly, unable to believe that he could be so angry.

"But we need the money right now! I'm laid up," he said, banging his hand on the plaster on his leg, "remember?"

That afternoon I took Fudge for a walk, and left Paul staring dismally into the fire.

As I trudged along I knew something was going badly wrong with our marriage. I curled my fingers into Fudge's fur, and remembered again the time when he'd been a puppy and there had been so much to look forward to.

Gloomily I looked down at Fudge. He must be — what? Twelve, now. It was impossible!

But Jamie was 12, I realised, so Fudge must be. I noticed for the first time he'd put on weight, was breathless after a long walk, and he didn't run gaily along the riverbank any more.

Tears caught at my throat. If Fudge went, I knew a part of me and my marriage went, too.

When I went back home Paul and I patched things up. I smothered my pride and went back to the Flower Pot because I hadn't realised he counted quite so much on my money. After all, we weren't that hard up, I reasoned. And it was then a terrible thought had struck me — Paul had met someone else . . .

Hurriedly I pushed the thought away — or was I refusing to face it?

Anyway from then on I made an even greater effort to keep the house shining, cook good meals and make sure the children behaved themselves when Paul was around.

For quite some time we lived in a sort of vacuum — everyone was being very polite to everyone else, but although we struggled on, I knew it couldn't last.

And it didn't.

ONE Saturday four months ago Paul came to me and instinctively I knew what he was going to say, just by looking at his set face. Jamie was on a Scouts' outing and Carol at dancing classes, so we were on our own for once.

Oddly enough, I'd been looking forward to that morning — just the two of us.

I'd made sandwiches and scones, and I planned to have lunch on the patio if the weather was fine. I watched the sun peep out from behind fluffy, white clouds and began to set the tray.

Continued on page 27

MACBETH –
The Cat That Ruled My Life

I had no illusions about him. That cat was a bad-tempered bully and a tyrant. Then came the day it seemed he'd gone out of my life for ever!

A FEW weeks after celebrating his twentieth birthday, Macbeth stalked out into the garden, laid himself down in the middle of the herbaceous border, and quietly expired.

The odious Macbeth had insinuated himself into our household one summer's evening more than two decades ago. He was borne into my

By ANNA MILFORD

life in the ecstatic arms of Stephen, who had won him at the church fête.

Nothing I could say would part him from his trophy. No threats, no bribes, would separate him from his cuddly prize and short of tearing the creature from his grasp, there was nothing I could do.

The kitten was a minute bundle of black fur with a tiny pointed face marked with a white blaze. He would have looked very appealing gazing out from the pages of a calendar, and there, in my opinion, was where he belonged, not in my house.

Robert, my elder son, had always insisted on Shakespearean names for the family pets, and promptly called him Macbeth.

I also knew my Bard, and remarked sourly that he would be better named after one of the "secret, black and midnight hags" or their familiar Paddock. These suggestions were ignored and Macbeth he became.

Every cliché ever coined about ingratitude and contempt for one's benefactor applied to that creature's attitude to me. He bit the hand that fed him; he accepted every privilege as his due and accepted no responsibility in return.

We had had a variety of pets over the years, living out their lives in peace and contentment within the family circle and then quietly dying at the end of their allotted span of years. White mice, gerbils, hamsters, guinea pigs, and naturally dogs. All had lived and died with us. They were loved, mourned, and after a little while replaced, but none of them had lingered on into grotesque old age like Macbeth.

We had got through three dogs in the past twenty years. Hamlet, the melancholy Bassett-hound, had been followed by the evil-tempered dachshund, Iago, and now our labrador, gentle Banquo, was having his days made a misery by the lifestyle of Kommandant Macbeth.

The wretched animal imposed on the dog's good nature at every turn. Sleeping in his box when the fancy took him; eating his dinner; tearing up his rug and chasing his friends out of the garden. A miniscule fraction of Banquo's size, he yet managed to take up the entire hearthrug leaving the shivering labrador to huddle forlornly in the shadow of the coal scuttle on winter nights.

THE YOUNG ONES

Most weekends, my husband and I go to stay with an old aunt who is in her eighties.

We always enjoy seeing her, but what really makes our day is when she shouts up the stairs on a Sunday morning:

"Do you kids want a cup of tea in bed?"

Considering both my husband and I are in our late fifties, that's quite a compliment!

It might have been thought that the dog's patient humility would be a shining example to Macbeth, but such is the nature of tyrants and bullies that the more the victim silently endures his torments the greater the indignities heaped upon him.

It was not as if he could ascribe his great age to having lived a virtuous and temperate life. He had fought and terrorised every tom within a ten-mile radius and now had half a tail, rather less than that of his left ear and about a dozen other dishonourable scars.

In the pursuit of love he had

ranged far and wide and I saw innumerable traces of that distinctive white blaze spread across the county unto the third and fourth generation. His scavenging and pilfering forays were notorious in the neighbourhood and his behaviour to lesser, helpless creatures like small birds was as gluttonous as it was repellent.

I never saw him show the slightest sign of affection for anyone, though my husband, sons and later grandchildren all adored him and were convinced that my frequently expressed detestation of the creature was all a pose and like them I really loved him dearly.

"After all," they chorused, "it's you who buys and cooks his food. You who cleans out his basket. You who looks after him when we're away."

Even the local police suffered from the same delusion and gave me similar answers when yet again I went to retrieve Macbeth from the police station.

"Knocked down by a car he was, ma'am," the sergeant explained apologetically as if it had been his fault. "Left him for dead by the roadside, callous brute."

"And why was he not left there for good?" I demanded wrathfully, only to be excused by the sergeant's indulgent chuckle.

"Come, come, ma'am, we know you don't mean that. Quite a local legend it is, your devotion to this old fellow. We'd miss him too if he ever came to the end of his nine lives."

Unwillingly I took the exhausted cat home, and that was one of his last adventures before I found him in the garden stretched lifeless at my feet.

If revenge is said to be so sweet why did it turn to dust and ashes on my tongue? For with tears pouring down my face I gathered up the pathetic bundle of bones and dingy fur and carried it into the house.

I LAID Macbeth gently on the kitchen table and went sadly to the boot cupboard to find a suitable shoe box for a coffin. Dragging one from the back of a shelf, I dislodged a pile of old books, and when they came to rest on the floor a tattered manual of First Aid was open on top of the heap.

I was brought up short by a vivid diagram of the Kiss of Life.

The Kiss of Life! Of course, the very thing.

Book in hand, I dashed back to the kitchen to resurrect the dead.

"First turn the victim on his back." Right, except I soon discovered that a cat has no back to speak of, merely a knobbly spine with no supporting pads of flesh. I tried to balance Macbeth's paws upwards but as soon as I released him he flopped over limp and flabby as a beanbag. Eventually I wedged him between the toaster and a hefty cookery book and read on.

"Wipe any foreign matter from the mouth and ensure the tongue is not blocking the throat."

I was lavish with the use of kitchen paper and was glad to find Macbeth's pointed tongue in its usual place, and then bravely attempted the instructions regarding the actual mechanics of resuscitation.

"Keep up a continuous rhythm," the book continued. "People have been resuscitated after a considerable period and there should be, if possible, relays of first aiders to maintain the treatment for as long as three hours. In the case of a single operator not less than half an hour should be attempted."

Sucking, blowing and squeezing, I struggled on, when suddenly, unbelievably, I felt a flutter in the chest beneath my hands. I stepped back to rest a moment and it was as well I did. The erstwhile victim took a precipitate leap to the floor and sprawled in a panting heap on the lino. I scooped him up and laid him in his favourite chair and fetched a saucer of milk.

He sniffed it and turned his face to the wall. I dipped my finger in the milk and held it to his mouth and was smartly nipped for my pains. Clearly the beast was returning to normal, although I dared not allow myself to think I had won too easily. He was capable of dying again just to spite me.

Grudgingly I fetched the brandy bottle and poured out a stingy measure of our precious duty-free. Using a spoon this time, I tempted him with a few drops. After a cautious lick he perked up astonishingly and pushing the spoon aside, shoved his tongue into the cup and lapped noisily, pausing every now and then with his head on one side as if savouring the bouquet.

After relishing the last expensive mouthful he stretched luxuriously and stepped down from the chair and made for his dinner bowl by the back door.

Swaying alarmingly and placing his paws with the exaggerated precision of a stage drunk he wove a tortuous way across the room.

Negotiating a return journey to the comforts of the chair proved too hazardous and after half a dozen tottering steps he subsided into a pie-eyed heap and lay there snoring for the rest of the day. Occasionally his sottish trance was disturbed by drunken hiccups but otherwise he slept like the dead.

Macbeth has profited from his brush with death. Every now and then he will "come over queer" and sink down pathetically, indicating to even the most flinty-hearted that his last hour has come. Refusing all nourishment, he will lie gasping pitifully until the bottle of Five Star is produced and a generous measure poured down his throat. Then to everyone's incredulous delight, he will miraculously recover.

Only one person is totally unimpressed by this act. Macbeth knows that I am already regretting my all-too-successful efforts at re-animation, but he dare not push his luck too far. The last time he played his brandy trick on my gullible family I gave him a piece of my mind, and if looks could kill — I would have been the one in need of the Kiss of Life. ■

Continued from page 22

Then Paul came into the kitchen and as soon as I saw him I knew something was wrong.

"Holly, I want to talk to you," he said firmly.

And, I realised, he never called me darling any more. It was always Holly — as though the girl he'd married didn't exist any more.

I had to put off the moment. Hastily I grabbed at straws.

"I'm just making tea," I babbled. "The kettle's just boiled. I thought we'd have it on the patio."

"Not now, Holly, I *have* to talk to you."

Silently then I followed him into the sitting-room. Absent-mindedly my gaze took in the room and I thought, with pride, how lovely it looked — how homely.

"Holly." Paul stood with his back to me, looking out at the sun-flooded garden. "Holly," he said, "I'm leaving, I'm sorry."

"Leaving?" I couldn't get my breath. I leaned against a chair, trying to take in what he'd said. "What do you mean, Paul?"

He turned slowly. "Look, Holly, there's not much left between us, is there? All you seem to think about is buying things for the house, a new carpet, new chairs."

He paused. "The house has become your god, Holly. Even the kids don't bring in friends any more. They go to them instead. Or hadn't you noticed?"

I had. But I thought it was because they were growing up, away from us. They were that age, Jamie was 16, Carol 14.

I hit back furiously. "Who stopped them playing their records the other day! They went round to Roger's that very evening!"

"That's unfair and you know it!" Paul returned. "Surely we're entitled to a little peace!

"The point is, Holly, *you* just don't seem to care any more. You go off to your flower shop, take Fudge for his walks. You don't — communicate any more."

"How can I!" I stormed. "You're never here to communicate with! You're always out, or you've got your head in a book, or you're watching TV. And *you* were the one who wanted me to carry on working! I don't get the chance to communicate with you any more!"

I paused, almost afraid of what I was going to say next. "Are you sure this isn't just an excuse?" I went on. "Aren't you to blame? Have you met someone else — someone you think may give you more out of life?"

To my utter horror he looked away. "No, I don't think so."

"You don't *think* so!" I said, and now all my fears and doubts were true. This *was* the end. There was someone else, there must be.

"Why have you been so distant, so uncaring, lately," I went on, probing, "if there isn't anyone else, Paul?"

It was true. For weeks he hadn't even kissed me goodbye before going off in the morning. I'd struggled on, trying not to let him know how hurt I'd been.

He turned to me angrily.

"There isn't anyone else, Holly! I think —" He hesitated. "I think there could be, if I let it happen. Put it that way. But I don't want it to!

"I've been hanging on, hoping things would change, but it's no good. All you care about is the bits and pieces you buy — your new curtains and . . ." His voice tailed off.

The hurt spread, filling me so I could hardly speak.

A Child's-Eye View

IT'S every gardener's dream. A rich, green lawn, smooth as a billiard table, unsullied by weeds and with edges sharp and clean.

Until this year The Man of the House was no exception. Though to describe him as a gardener is probably an over-statement.

Needless to say, he never achieved it. It wasn't for the lack of trying. He did try — for about a fortnight — every year.

Dressings, regular cutting, plenty of water — his methods were straight out of the text books.

The trouble was, the text books tell you that you must have staying power and this he doesn't have.

Once the golf season got into full swing, and the weeds began really to "mean business," they invariably won.

After that it was a sigh, a shake of the head and a quick cut with the mower.

But this year there has been no determined effort and no regrets. And it's all because of something that happened at the end of last summer.

He was about to give the grass a cursory cut when a freckled face appeared over the hedge. It was Jill, the little girl from down the road.

"I like your grass," she said.

"Do you?" he said.

"Yes, it's the nicest in the whole street. All the rest are plain old green and yours is covered with lovely daisies and dandelions."

Since that moment we've both seen our lawn in a completely new light — through the eyes of a child.

"Don't you understand, Paul?" I said, tears welling inside me. "There didn't seem to be anything else. I have to have something to live for, and you don't seem to need me any more. Even the children are growing up, away from us. Jamie will be at art school next term, had you forgotten?"

I stared out the window unseeingly. Fudge was coming rheumatically over to the french door. He stood outside, and automatically I went to let him in.

Paul sighed. "'Leave him out there, Holly. It won't hurt him!"

Deliberately, I opened the door and Fudge came in, touching my hand with his nose on the way.

I turned to Paul, tears trickling slowly down my cheeks.

"At least he needs me, Paul!" I whispered. "Sometimes I've felt he cares more about me than you do. Now it seems I was right!"

PAUL left early the next day with a suitcase. He would, he informed me, call for the rest of his things one afternoon, when I was out. It would be easier.

"All right," I said coldly. I'd not slept all night, my face felt numb from tears.

At breakfast Carol stared at me with 14-year-old concern.

"You all right, Mum? Can I do anything?" She looked so young, so vulnerable, in her jeans and T-shirt, my heart ached for her. I only hoped she wouldn't have to go through this when she grew up.

Then Jamie rushed into the kitchen.

"I'm late, Mum. I'll just have toast and marmalade." He grabbed a slice of toast, spread it rapidly, and pecked me on the cheek. "I'll be late tonight. Going to hear Roger's new LP. See you!"

It would be difficult for them, I thought. To realise that Paul had gone, wouldn't be coming back. But they were old enough to cope — perhaps understand a little.

Carol went to school, and I was alone. I knew suddenly I couldn't go to the Flower Pot. I had to hide here at home, away from curious eyes.

To a certain extent, I knew that Paul was right. I *had* become houseproud. And I got tired, so I grumbled at them all, even poor old Fudge.

Suddenly, staring at the empty kitchen, I didn't care any more. Paul, I thought with bitterness, would have to pay me something, would have to support the children till they left home. I would leave the Flower Pot and the money I'd thought Paul wanted me to earn, and do something I'd had at the back of my mind for a long time.

For a while I eyed my friends and neighbours suspiciously, wondering if it was one of them who'd taken Paul from me. Then I began going to a local art class. There were seven of us, and it was fun.

But I didn't have Paul to talk to, to tell him about the elderly man who painted nothing but railway stations, or the woman who painted her own portrait, incessantly.

I missed him so much it was always with me. Seventeen years is a long time to live together, then part. I couldn't bear the thought. But then something happened that brought all my unhappiness to a head. Fudge was taken ill . . .

That evening Carol came bursting into the sitting-room, where Jamie was lying on the floor surrounded by magazines and a cup of hot chocolate.

"Mum," she called out. "Come quickly, it's Fudge!"

My heart seemed literally to turn over.

I ran to the kitchen, but the minute I saw him I knew it was serious — very serious.

I phoned the vet and when we took Fudge to him, he shook his head.

"He's an old dog, Mrs Henley. I'm sorry, there's not much I can do."

★　　　★　　　★　　　★

Fudge died yesterday and ever since I've been carrying a wedge of grief around with me, unable to cry, to do anything.

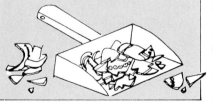

PARTY PIECES!

I was exhausted after preparing for our dinner party and when the meal was over I didn't relish the prospect of washing-up.

With a sigh, I turned towards the sink, wishing I could get back to my guests.

As I turned, my sleeve caught the edge of the tray of dirty dishes and every single one came crashing down!

What could I do? I just shovelled all the bits and pieces into the waste bin and went back to the party.

But I certainly won't be making any more wishes in the future — it's too expensive!

Carol cried all night and Jamie seemed lost in his own private thoughts.

Somehow I got through the morning and now I'm sitting out here in the sun.

I still can't believe Fudge has gone. Paul's face comes into my mind. I should tell him. He will be upset, I know, because he loved Fudge, too.

SUDDENLY there is a sound behind me and a shadow falls across the patio.

It is Paul. He looks down at me and suddenly it's as though he's never been away.

"How did you know?" I whisper, and he touches my shoulder very gently.

"Jamie phoned the office," he says quietly.

"I can't believe it's really happened . . ."

"No, it's hard, I know," he replies, then stands silent for a moment.

He looks round the garden and something comes into his face. He smiles gently.

"You might have kept the roses pruned," he says.

30

"I — I'm not bothering about the house quite so much these days."

"So Jamie tells me. I've been seeing him — Carol, too. You didn't know?" he asks, at my surprised face.

I shake my head, feeling oddly betrayed. Paul sits down on the patio beside me, almost shyly.

"They tell me — you've changed," he adds. "I must say the sitting-room doesn't look the way it used to."

I remember I haven't even tidied it today. Since the news about Fudge all the heart has left me.

I stare at Paul, noting his hair is greyer, there are fine lines in his face I've never noticed before.

"And you?" I ask. "Have you changed at all?"

He touches my hand. "I never really did change, Holly. I just — wanted to matter to you more than anything, or anyone."

"The girl?" I ask, and he shakes his head tiredly.

"There was nothing. Perhaps I was trying to make you believe that someone cared, even if you didn't."

Suddenly there's an odd sound from the sitting-room, and Paul gets hurriedly to his feet, an anxious expression on his face. He looks down at me, then disappears.

I sit here, looking at the garden, and for the first time the sun seems warm on my face.

Then I turn, and Paul is standing there, with a small bundle in his arms. A squirming bundle with long floppy ears and huge brown eyes, only this time the pup is the colour of burned toffee.

My eyes fill with tears, and he puts the puppy into my arms.

"I couldn't bear to think of you without a dog," he says, and his voice is unsteady. The puppy wriggles, and then my tears come, and I weep for Fudge, and for Paul and for myself.

Paul puts his arms round me and hugs both me and the puppy to him.

"Holly, can't we start again?" he says. "You and me and the puppy?"

I feel oddly at peace. The puppy struggles from my arms and wobbles on bandy legs to Fudge's basket. He climbs untidily into it then collapses, a bundle of fur, panting, eyes fixed on us.

Then he turns round two or three times and settles down in the sun. He's come home.

So has Paul. I turn to him, and nod, stammering between my sobs.

"We'll have to call him Toffee!" I say stupidly. "He's just like a lump of burned toffee."

Paul's lips are on my hair, and the puppy whimpers.

I think of Fudge and his loyalty and love, and the puppy suddenly staggers out of the basket and comes over to me.

I touch his ears gently, and smile. My tears are over now, it is time to make a new start.

——————— * **THE END** * ———————

I Always Was A Soft

Ladies! Do you want to earn extra money in your spare time? Then don't come to me for advice, says Mary Hooper . . .

WHILE not wishing to put others off trying to earn a little extra money, I have to report that the only fund my own puny efforts increased is a fund of funny stories to tell friends.

Market Research was my first notion. It seemed the ideal job, with flexible hours to suit myself. Unfortunately, the assignments were practically impossible!

"Quota to find," began my instructions on a survey about household cleansers. "Three housewives under 25; three over 25 and under 50 and five over 50. Three to be in lower-income bracket, three in upper-income bracket."

It was easy enough at first, but after I had crossed off the younger element I knocked and ding-donged for ages before I could find the over-50 lot.

Also you need a mind like a computer to work out exactly what sort of person you need when you are almost at the end of a survey: "One under 25, middle income; one over 50, lower income," I would mutter to myself as I trotted down the road.

Sometimes I didn't find out until the end of forty massively trivial questions like, "How long does your scouring powder take to flush away?" that a woman I had earmarked as a 35-year-old upper-income was really a sophisticated 23-year-old married to a refuse collector.

I think I lasted for two surveys before I found them just too exasperating.

My next venture was started by a friend's casual remark that, "the Americans will pay anything for brass rubbings." Before you could say "Mediaeval Church Brass" there I was equipped with heel ball and graph paper, madly rubbing the brasses in a nearby church.

Every time anyone entered the church I would stuff my rolled-up rubbings under the nearest pew. I had paid my fee, but you aren't supposed to take rubbings for profit.

I recall a certain vicar coming in for the second time one afternoon and remarking kindly, "Still at it?" I went scarlet and murmured something about doing the beautiful brass justice.

I was duly punished, though, because I didn't sell a single rubbing as no-one actually told me where to find the Americans.

I did try to sell them to a smart art shop, but the well-bred assistant merely glanced scathingly at my offerings and waved towards a wall covered in beautiful ormolu-framed brass rubbings.

Touch!

By
MARY
HOOPER

I THEN decided to try something more in keeping with my image — soft-toy making. I took delivery of bags of stuffing and limp, dead-looking animals. The man assured me I could earn pounds in just an evening.

I timed my first animal to coincide with my toddler's daytime sleep, and gaily rushed into the dining-room to start earning real money. An hour-and-a-half later I was still fighting to get stuffing down an elephant's trunk — not that he could even stand up properly — and the room was covered in tiny pieces of kapok.

I made a thin and wild-looking cat in two hours that evening, then gave it up as a bad job.

My most spectacular failure was as a "lingerie party lady." Again, this was described in glowing terms by the lady manager.

"Some of my gels earn £60 a week," she assured me. I was full of hope when she brought my kit round.

"All it needs is a press, dear — someone had to leave suddenly," the manageress explained.

At last, I thought, this was it —

Continued overleaf.

the way to my fortune! I persuaded four friends to start me off by having parties for me, and rehearsed my speech. Every garment had a name and I had to know it; my husband sat for HOURS while I picked up each garment in turn with a gay, "This is Jezebel, ladies; a super little number that is sure to be a hit with the men, ha, ha." Every so often he would say gloomily, "Wrong again; that was Salome," and I would have to start all over again.

I got to my first party an hour early and had reached the hysterical giggling stage by the time the first guests (they're never "customers") arrived.

My friend wasn't much help for she vanished into the kitchen while I did my piece. Apparently, she couldn't bear to watch.

Suffice to say that her lack of confidence in me was not unfounded: I muddled the garments, calling them by all the wrong names and generally making a hash of things. I sold a grand total of £4 worth of clothes that evening.

My next party a few days later featured a stripper who, as I held up flimsy bras and slips, insisted on stripping down to her pants and trying them on.

"What do you think of this?" she would demand, prancing up and down with various items of my not-yet-paid-for kit.

The answer from the audience was, predictably, "Not much — seen cheaper in town," or "Fancy only selling it in that colour."

Since then, I haven't had the nerve to try anything else, although yesterday I did see an advert for a marvellous little job. It was sewing buttons on cards and sounded dead easy . . . ∎

34

"SOMETHING," Russell Neilson announced to his mother on Saturday morning, "will have to be done about it!"

His mother glanced up from the letter she was writing and nodded approvingly.

"Quite right. I've written to Mr Marchant three times now about that rubbish tip at Brackley Head, and do you know, he hasn't even bothered to reply!"

She frowned. "I would have thought you might have been able to put in a word about it, Russell," she added almost accusingly. "You are on the board now, after all."

Tactfully Russell refrained from explaining that it had been on his advice Peter Marchant, the company chairman, had ignored his mother's letters.

He sighed. Having a mother like his really did make life difficult. Luckily Peter Marchant had been remarkably understanding about it — and had even showed some interest in the matter.

"Your mother certainly seems concerned about it all," the older man had mused. And Russell had stepped into the breach.

"Well, she — she's getting on a bit, Mr Marchant," he'd explained weakly without conviction.

Peter Marchant had smiled. "Aren't we all?" he'd asked, then sighed easily. "You're a bright young director, Russell. Thank you for coming to see me."

Now, Russell looked at his mother, her head bent once more over the sheet of paper, and smiled in spite of his irritation.

Other people had mothers who knitted bedsocks, or made rugs, or ran church bazaars. But not him.

Oh, no, his mother had to devote her energies to cleaning up the world, and, in particular, the village of Teversleigh.

It wouldn't have been so bad even
f she had confined her attentions to
tter, like in previous campaigns.
But now she was waging a war
gainst the factory of which he had
ecently been appointed a director —
nd all because of a silly little bit of
vasteground that wasn't doing any-
ne the least bit of harm!

Admittedly it wasn't very pretty,
ut what the Teversleigh Anti-
'ollution League — or whatever it
vas the bunch of cranks called them-
elves — didn't understand was the
ost that clearing it would involve,
ot to mention finding an alternative
lace for the disposal of scrap.

**Complete Story By
SARAH BURKHILL**

He had his route to the top all mapped out —
until he ran into . . .

Those Dangerous Curves

35

Russell sighed again, and as he looked out of the window, he remembered what he had really been saying to his mother.

"I didn't mean something would have to be done about the tip at Brackley Head," he went on. "I meant something would have to be done about *that*!" He pointed dramatically at the car that was parked outside his driveway.

His mother followed his gesture.

"What's the matter, dear?" she asked concernedly. "Is something wrong with Barbara's car?"

"Everything! I mean just look at the flowers she's painted on it!" Russell spluttered, then quickly regained his composure. "However, that isn't my concern. What *is* is the fact that she's got it parked outside our drive again!"

"Well, it's too near the corner if she leaves it at her own gate," his mother said defensively.

Russell glared at her. He knew she had grown fond of Barbara Maxwell. Quite apart from anything else, the girl was also an ardent anti-pollutionist, and he had no doubt his mother saw her as a comrade-in-arms. But really —

"I don't know what you're getting so upset about," his mother went on. "Since you were made a director, you've become remarkably stuffy. The car's not doing you any harm, Rusty."

Russell winced at his mother's pet name for him.

"It is!" he retorted. "It's stopping me getting my car out."

"But you're not going anywhere, dear," his mother pointed out logically.

Russell grunted. "That's not the point," he said patiently. "I might want to go somewhere, and if I did, I couldn't.

"Anyway, as a matter of fact I *am* going out."

He resisted the temptation to add "So there!" and went to fetch his jacket.

He had to sound his car horn three times before Barbara Maxwell came reluctantly out of her house.

"Sorry, have I blocked you in again?" she asked brightly.

Russell wound down the window as she approached.

"For the fifth time this week," he said irately.

"I'm terribly sorry. Really I am." She smiled winningly and Russell almost melted.

If she hadn't been one of the anti-pollution brigade, he might have melted far enough to smile back. But she was, and he didn't.

Instead he uttered a slightly mollified grunt and watched in silence as Barbara moved her heap out of the way.

He sat fuming. The inconvenience was only part of the reason he objected so much to her parking. What concerned him more was the fact that somebody might think the "thing" belonged to him!

He shuddered at the mental picture of Peter Marchant seeing it at his door. The hump-backed little motor car had originally been white, but Barbara's none-too-artistic hand had painted pink and blue

WEDDING ENSEMBLE

I'll always look back with pleasure and amusement to my granddaughter's wedding.

The bride's mother, whose youngest child was 14, had discovered she was pregnant again. Her dad had been involved in a motor-cycling accident and had his foot in plaster.

The other grandmother and I had a little giggle about this. We could just imagine a report of the wedding.

"The bride wore a pretty white outfit, the bride's mother wore a maternity dress, and the bride's father came on crutches!"

flowers over most of its surface area, and the name "Pansy" on the bonnet.

Russell snorted and slid his sports car into first gear.

"Oh, hang on a minute," Barbara called out as he was about to turn into the street.

He braked abruptly.

"Has your mother told you about the demonstration?" she asked pleasantly.

Russell poked his head out of the window.

"The *what*?" he asked suspiciously.

"Didn't you know? Well, we're having a demonstration at the factory next week — about the rubbish tip," she informed him. "It was your mother's idea, of course. Frightfully *involved* person. You should be proud of her."

FOR the hundredth time, Mother, you're not going!" Russell said firmly the following Friday night as his mother, armed with a paintbrush, was putting the finishing touches to her demonstration placard.

"Hush, dear," his mother replied with equal firmness. "Can't you see we're busy?"

But Barbara merely smiled sweetly and said nothing.

Russell sighed with exasperation and turned his gaze to Barbara Maxwell. The girl had come in for a last-minute briefing, and she was another reason he felt a show of authority was called for.

Russell opened his mouth a few times before any words came out. "But there's no *point* in doing that, Mother," he tried to explain. "You won't be there! I'll — I'll —"

"You'll what, dear?" his mother asked kindly.

Russell thought frantically. "I'll — I'll leave home!" he announced grimly. It was the ultimate threat. The last time he had used it he had been six years old, and armed with a packet of ginger snap biscuits and Thread-Bear, his much-loved and much-worn teddy.

His threat didn't work, however — not then, and not the following morning. For by the time Russell got out of bed, his mother was already gone.

Pyjama-clad, he paced up and down the living-room. It was downright deceitful, he thought, sneaking off like that when he was still in bed. He glanced out of the window and saw that the "flower-mobile" wasn't in the roadway, and grunted.

Of course, that dratted reporter must have taken her off! His mother, he tried to convince himself, would never have behaved with such outright defiance if it hadn't been for Barbara Maxwell . . .

Donning trousers and a sweater, he decided that positive action was called for. He would drive out to the factory right now and put a stop to this nonsense, he thought.

The Anti-Pollution League could do as they pleased, within the law, but he was definitely not having his mother parading up and down, making a fool of herself. He would remove her — bodily if necessary!

Encouraged by this new decisiveness, he set out.

THE factory wasn't a great distance away, and Russell abandoned his car on the street opposite before marching resolutely up to the gate.

Of all the ridiculous ideas, he thought incredulously. A crowd of grown-up men and women behaving like rebellious teenagers! Several of the group paced back and forth with placards, while others sat awkwardly across the entrance.

Barbara Maxwell, standing chatting on the pavement, saw him and waved.

"Hi, Rusty. Come to join us?" she called brightly.

He glared ferociously at her and began his struggle through the group. He had caught a glimpse of his mother at the rear, and a mere 50 prone bodies were not going to prevent him reaching her.

"Can't you just sit at the edge?" an elderly woman, whose foot he had trod on, demanded. "You should have got here earlier if you wanted a good place."

Russell murmured an apology and announced irately that he had no intention of sitting anywhere. Really, it was a pity he had been quite so emphatic about this, for after narrowly avoiding treading on a hand, he found himself sprawled inelegantly on the ground.

"Hey, this is a peaceful protest!" the man next to him complained as Russell struggled to get to his feet.

"Stop causing trouble, young man!" a woman said and poked him with her umbrella, causing him to fall heavily once more into the mass of bodies.

Russell yelped.

"Of course, you always get the hooligan element at these things," he heard a voice saying above him. "Gets those of us who are genuinely concerned a bad name."

With a supreme effort he managed to get himself out of the tangle. But he could feel his anger rising. That he, Russell Neilson, a director of Marchant's Manufacturers and a peaceful, law-abiding citizen, should be subjected to this was insufferable!

"Now look here!" he began, then somebody bumped into him, and he threw out his arms to keep his balance — and felt his fist connect with something hard.

"No," a voice said warningly. "*You* look here."

Russell gulped. The hard object his fist had come in contact with was the helmet of a local policeman, and the face underneath it wasn't in the least friendly. Neither was the hand that gripped his shoulder.

"But you don't understand, officer," he protested as the hand ushered him through the crowd. "I'm Russell Neilson, and I'm perfectly —"

"Just keep moving, there's a good fellow," the policeman said evenly. "We'll get your name and address at the station."

"Don't be ridiculous!" Russell shouted. Hysteria was setting in. "You can't possibly think I'm one of them! I tell you I'm Russell Neilson —"

"One more word and I'll have you for resisting arrest, too," the officer told him.

Russell shut up and allowed himself to be trotted meekly off to the awaiting van.

THE flower-mobile was parked outside the police station when Russell finally convinced the officers inside of his innocence. Barbara Maxwell hovered at the door.

Russell walked towards her. He would have been quite touched at the concern on her face, had it not been that the whole thing was mostly her fault.

"Got it all cleared up then, Rusty?" she asked sympathetically.

"Russell," he replied coldly. "Or better still, Mr Neilson."

"Oh, don't be so pompous. Your mother thought you looked rather upset when you — er — left, so I've come to give you a lift home. Hop in."

She held the passenger door open and smiled at him.

Russell scowled. "If you think I'm riding around town in a car called 'Pansy' you've got another think coming!" he exclaimed indignantly.

But Barbara had pranced into the driver's seat and was now revving the engine impatiently.

"Well, you'll have to if you want to get home. The police have towed your car away," she said, then added, "It was causing an obstruction."

Russell opened his mouth then closed it again quickly. Reluctantly he got into the car — after a hasty glance up and down the street to make sure he was unobserved.

"Hey, where do you think you're going?" he asked suspiciously,

Getting In The Swim

"YOU can't swim?" My friend, Margaret, looked at me in amazement. "Oh, we must do something about that."

Before I knew it, she had steamrollered me into agreeing to go with her to the local swimming baths the following day.

Off she went, happily thinking she was doing me a good turn. While I was left, deep in thought — a long-forgotten fear stirring inside me.

Suddenly my thoughts went winging back to my childhood, and the long summer breaks from school.

It always happened — one day someone in the neighbourhood "gang" would suggest going to the baths and, not wanting to be the odd one out, I'd tag along.

The bus journey was always a noisy, cheerful affair — for everyone but me. I sat silently clutching my towel and costume, thinking of the ordeal ahead.

The worst moment was stepping through the door of the baths. It was the sound first — the echoing shouts and splashes. Then, as I went through the door of the pool itself, that smell! That so-distinctive scent of the water.

Any resolve I'd mustered would drain away.

Do you know, when I went with Margaret the following day, it was exactly the same? I felt just as insecure.

But I learned two things that were different. I was taller for a start and the water at the shallow end wasn't so frightening. And Margaret was a marvellous teacher.

By the end of our session I was actually enjoying myself.

I'm not swimming yet, but I'm going again next week.

Who knows. Maybe it's still not too late to learn.

after they'd been travelling for a few minutes. "Home, in case you have forgotten, is that way."

He pointed back the way they'd come, feeling annoyed with himself for not having noticed sooner. The fact that Barbara's profile was much nicer to look at than the streets of town was not an adequate excuse.

"I thought we might take a run up to Brackley Head and have a look at the tip," Barbara explained innocently.

"Oh no you don't. You'll stop this instant, do you hear?" Russell said heatedly.

Barbara pulled in immediately to the side of the road.

"It'll be a marvellous story," she remarked conversationally as he reached for the door handle.

Russell's hand stopped in mid-air.

"*What* will be a marvellous story?" he asked against his better judgment — and the sudden feeling that it might be better if he didn't know.

"How a director of Marchant's Manufacturers got run in at a demo," Barbara said wickedly, confirming his worst suspicions.

"You wouldn't!" Russell said emphatically. Then with a note of hope in his voice, "You wouldn't? You know perfectly well how it happened. It would be against all the ethics of your profession to make it seem otherwise."

Barbara grinned smugly and he got the impression that where her pet subject of pollution was concerned she might not be too ethical.

He groaned and sank back into the seat, and Barbara started off once more.

"AREN'T the trees lovely?" she remarked lightly when they had travelled a short way out of town. "I couldn't believe my luck, landing this job on *The Herald* and getting out of London. Don't you adore the countryside?"

Russell sniffed. In his opinion once you'd seen one tree you'd seen them all, but he glanced about him anyway. Funny, the leaves had turned much the same colour as Barbara's hair, a sort of russety-gold. Rather pretty, really, he thought, without knowing whether he meant the hair or the leaves, or both.

"I've been going through the old newspaper files, trying to get some information on the place," Barbara said. "Did you know that Brackley Head used to be a favourite spot for picnics?"

Russell squirmed uncomfortably.

"And for lovers," Barbara continued after a pause. "Especially in spring when all the wild daffodils were out. There used to be masses of them — down there." She drew to a halt and pointed.

Russell swallowed and looked down on to the Marchant Scrap Pile.

"Quite a change from the daffodils," she remarked pleasantly.

"We-ell. Yes. Yes, I suppose it is." He had no option but to agree.

"And wouldn't it be so much nicer if we could get rid of that lot and get the daffodils back?"

"Mmm, yes, I suppose so." Russell nodded uncertainly.

"And you're going to see to it for us, aren't you, Rusty?"

She turned enormous, trusting eyes on him, and Russell found himself nodding before the full import of her question dawned.

"Now wait a minute!" he began, forgetting even to object to the "Rusty." "There's nothing I can do about it! I'm only a very junior member of the board, and I can't go stirring up trouble for the sake

Continued on page 47

A brush with the UNKNOWN

The world of show business seems especially prone to visitations by spectral beings . . .

By JILLIAN HENDERSON

STORIES are rife in Theatreland of entertainers who simply cannot leave the thrill of show business — even after they pass away.

One of the most well-known stories is that of the Man in Grey, who reputedly haunts the famous Theatre Royal, in London's Drury Lane. The unknown gent wears distinctive 18th-century clothes and is said to appear in the upper circle. His appearance is believed to herald a good run for the show taking place.

At the Haymarket Theatre, the spirit of an actor/manager by the name of J. B. Buckstone appears in one of the dressing-rooms, and this also promises a long and successful run.

A multi-talented showlady of the Victorian era, known as Fanny Kelly, is believed to have kept a constant vigil at the old Royalty Theatre in Soho for a good many years. She disappeared when the site was redeveloped for office blocks in the 1920s.

Many famous people claim have had a brush with the unknow

The unnerving experience Kojak actor, Telly Savalas, is qui well known. Driving through Lo Island, New York, in the ear hours of the morning over 30 yea ago, Telly ran out of petrol.

Searching on foot for a servi station, he was taken by surpri when a gentleman in a bla limousine pulled up to offer assi tance. He took him to the neare garage, loaned him the money f

Telly Savalas

some fuel and dropped him back at his car.

At this point, Telly insisted that his Samaritan write down his name and address so that he could repay his kindness. The gentleman obliged and the two parted company.

At a later date, when Telly called at the address his rescuer had supplied, he was shocked to discover that the man had been dead for three years. His widow even confirmed that the writing was that of her late husband.

Derek Jameson and his wife Ellen

ANOTHER celebrity who has experienced some uncanny incidents is housewives' favourite, Derek Jameson. His wife, Ellen, says, "These things are always happening around Derek!"

Friends for a good many years of psychic medium Doris Stokes, Derek and Ellen are firm believers in things supernatural.

Derek recalls one particularly eerie incident which began while he was walking in the pouring rain one afternoon in Manchester. Looking for shelter, Derek entered a church only to discover that a spiritualist meeting was in full swing.

He sat down at the back and within minutes was singled out by the medium chairing the proceedings.

She reminded him of a time, some years previously, when he was on guard duty. Two of his cronies had decided to take one of the military ambulances for a joyride, despite the fact that the bodies of two young men who had perished in a road traffic accident were in the back of the vehicle.

Derek said, "You can't treat the dead like that!" but he was laughed down by his companions.

Years later, on that wet afternoon, the unfortunate accident victims had come back to thank Derek for his show of respect.

"It was just pure chance that Derek walked into that church at that time," Ellen says. "He hadn't planned it and nobody could have known where he'd end up, yet a specific message came through."

One Christmas, there was a

strange coincidence in the Jameson household. Just before Christmas 1988, Ellen bought a rather unusual Advent calendar. It featured a highly-coloured picture of a knight in flowing robes, surrounded by candles.

For some reason, Derek took a particular shine to the illustration and decided he'd like to buy the artwork. It was only when they looked for an address to write to that they spotted the name of the artist — it was A. Jameson.

More recently, when Ellen underwent major surgery in hospital, Derek reports that he was racked with pain throughout her ordeal.

Barbara Lott

BARBARA LOTT — who plays Timothy Lumsden's horrendous mother in the BBC sit-com "SORRY" — had a ghostly experience a few years ago when she and her husband, Harry, visited Paris.

The couple are keen historians, so they went on a tour of the dungeons where French aristocrats were held before being executed by Madame La Guillotine.

Barbara recalls, "Wandering through Marie Antoinette's cell, I was suddenly overcome by an extraordinary sense of horror — cold terror, as if all the fear and dread which the prisoners must have felt, was being screamed out at me."

She felt so terrible that she sought out Harry, who had also felt "the crawling sense of evil."

"Let's get out of here!" Barbara begged.

Harry agreed and the two of them sat for half an hour in a nearby church to regain their composure. Barbara says, "I'd never ever felt anything like it before — and I never, ever want to again."

By way of light relief, Norman Wisdom told me this amusing anecdote. "When I was about twelve years of age, I was at a Scout camp. One night, a group of us saw something white about one hundred yards away, moving about in a hedge in an eerie fashion.

"Eventually, one of the lads dared me to go and investigate. Not knowing what to expect, I went over to it and stood talking to it for a moment or two.

"When I rejoined the others, I explained that it was a friendly ghost that was too shy to join us for a bite to eat. I became a temporary hero. I never did tell them that it was a large sheet of newspaper caught on some barbed wire!" ■

The quotations on this page, page 96 and pages 124 and 125 are taken from Harrap's Book Of Humorous Quotations, edited by G. F. Lamb.

" And "
I Quote ...

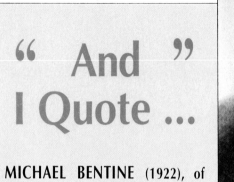

MICHAEL BENTINE (1922), of Peruvian extraction, was a leading British humorist after the war. He was one of the Goons in the programme's early years, and wrote material for many well-known comedians, besides presenting his own TV shows (e.g., *It's a Square World*).

One British Olympic sports commentator described a UK runner who was lagging far behind the field as: "Coming in confidently and supremely fit — a gallant sixteenth."

That roar of ecstatic welcome was for Her Royal Highness riding Kinky . . . Just coming up to the water jump . . . Good heavens, Kinky's **refused.** But Her Royal Highness has accepted! . . . What a brilliant swimmer she is!

"Have you any concrete evidence of ghosts?"
"No. Very few ghosts are made of concrete."

Tommy Trinder gave me invaluable advice about hecklers. "Always get them to repeat what they have said," he told me, "because nothing sounds quite so funny or offensive when it is repeated."

Our next-door neighbour turned out to be a funeral furnisher . . . During a bitterly cold winter he would lean over the garden fence. "Terrible weather," he'd say with a radiant smile. "They're dropping like flies."

Continued from page 41
of a few daffodils. Old Peter Marchant would think I'd gone off my head!"

"Ha!" She rounded on him. "That's it, you're afraid of Peter Marchant, aren't you?" she accused, grinning.

"No, I'm not," Russell said huffily. "It's just that — " He searched for a reason that wouldn't sound too cowardly. "Well, he is a very important man round here, isn't he?"

"You make him sound like an ogre." Barbara smiled. "I met him at a cocktail party last week, and he seemed rather sweet. Anyway, you could just sort of broach the subject, couldn't you, Rusty? That wouldn't do any harm."

"You mean, unless I do you're going to spread a libellous story about me all over the newspapers. That's blackmail!"

Barbara looked hurt. "Don't be silly, of course I wouldn't. I was only joking about that."

She turned the car round and headed back to town.

"I just thought that if you understood about Brackley Head, if you could visualise it as it would be cleared up, you might want to help. So I was wrong."

She shrugged sadly and Russell fought back the desire to put an arm round her and tell her that he'd see Peter Marchant first thing on Monday. That he'd clear the tip single-handed if only she'd smile at him like she had done a few moments before.

He shook himself and forced his attention to the street ahead. It must be the delayed shock, he thought. Strong black coffee was what he needed.

Nevertheless, he sneaked another glance at his driver.

"I'll let you park your *car* in front of my drive, though, if you like," he offered magnanimously. "I know I've been a bit —"

He broke off, a look of horror on his face. "Oh no, it's Peter Marchant!"

He slid down in the seat before the man on the opposite side of the road could catch a glimpse of him and his strange mode of transport.

"So it is," Barbara agreed, brightening. "See, I told you that you were frightened of him."

She swung the car across the road and screeched to a stop.

"What are you doing?" Russell hissed.

"Well," she said, winding down the window. "If no-one else is going to brave the lion, I will!

MR Marchant!" Barbara called, waving.
    Peter Marchant turned and smiled.

"Ah, it's our new *Herald* reporter. Nice to see you again, my dear. I hope you're keeping busy."

"Actually, I've just been down at the factory — for the protest meeting, you know."

Russell pushed himself further down in his seat and awaited the
Continued on page 54

MAKING THE MOST OF MUSHROOMS

Mushrooms are versatile and available all year round. Use them in our quick-cook recipes for maximum flavour and texture.

STIR-FRYING is the latest and most fuel economising way of cooking. This technique probably began in Southern China and over the years it has spread across Asia to Britain. Stir-frying is particularly good for mushrooms. Cooked quickly, they retain their nutrients.

Stir-frying is the technique of sautéing small pieces of vegetable, meat or fish in very little oil. The food must be stirred and tossed continuously to cook evenly on all sides. The average stir-fry recipe takes less than 10 minutes to cook, but it is important that all the ingredients are prepared and chopped before cooking is commenced.

Originally, the stoves were funnel shaped with a circular opening. The cooking vessel was therefore wide and curved to fit snugly over the charcoal fire, and a fierce heat was required to maintain the correct cooking temperature in the carbon-steel pans generally used.

Today, woks are often made of stainless steel or aluminium, and the "fierce heat" requirement has given way to a rather less aggressive approach, thanks to modern materials and better manufacturing techniques. Modern woks have a flat base so that they are suitable for cooking on gas, electricity and solid fuel. (If you don't have a wok, a deep frying-pan can be substituted.)

For Perfect Results
1. Always assemble all ingredients. The vegetables and meat should be pre-cut, seasoned or marinated. Measure the spices, liquids and seasonings. Set everything out in order beside the stove.
2. Heat the dry, clean wok before you add the oil, then dribble the oil around the sides of the wok. Keep the heat fairly high to cook fast, but beware of any splattering which may occur when food is first added.
3. Firmly clasp the handle of the wok with one hand, and use the other hand to add the foods and toss them with a spatula.
4. Cook the foods which need longer cooking times first, e.g., meat and root vegetables. Then add the shorter cooking foods, e.g., mushrooms, later. Stir-fried vegetables should always be tender-crisp and not soggy. Never overcook them.
5. Add any liquids or seasoning sparingly.
6. Finally add the thickening agents — cornflour moistened to a paste with a little water, or peanut butter, and stir to a smooth, velvety texture.

SPICY STIR-FRIED KIDNEYS (Illustrated)

5-6 lambs' kidneys, halved and cores removed.
30 ml oil.
350 g small new potatoes, scrubbed and each cut into four.
175 g new carrots, scraped and thinly sliced.
225 g courgettes, thinly sliced.
225 g closed cup mushrooms, wiped and sliced.
1.25-2.5 ml hot chilli powder.
1 x 5 ml spoon turmeric.
1 x 5 ml spoon ground coriander.
Salt.

Make criss-cross cuts in a lattice pattern halfway through the thickness of each kidney.

Heat oil in a wok. Stir in kidneys and potatoes. Cover and cook for 5 minutes. Stir in carrots and courgettes. Cover and cook for 5 minutes. Stir in remaining ingredients plus 60 ml water, and continue to cook for 20 minutes, stirring occasionally.

Serves 4.

MUSHROOM STIR-FRY (Illustrated)

2 x 15 ml sesame seed oil.
175 g carrot, cut into strips.
1 green pepper, seeds removed and cubed.
225 g flat mushrooms, wiped and sliced.
227 g can sliced bamboo shoots, drained.
2 x 15 ml spoon light soy sauce.
2 x 15 ml spoon Hoi Sin sauce.
2 x 15 ml spoon stock.

Heat oil in a wok. Stir in carro green pepper, cover and cook fo 1 minute. Stir in mushrooms, cover an cook for 2 minutes, stirring occasio ally.

Add bamboo shoots, then gradual stir in remaining ingredients. Bring boil, simmer for 1 minute, then serv garnished with spring onion curls, liked.

Serves 4.

STIR-FRIED CHICKEN with PRAWNS
(Illustrated)

30 ml oil.
3 sticks celery, finely chopped.
½ large onion, sliced lengthways.
2 cloves garlic, crushed.
350 g open cup mushrooms, wiped and turned
275 g fresh chicken breast, cut into strips.
125 g peeled prawns.
Salt and pepper.
2 x 15 ml spoon lemon juice.
To Garnish:
Chopped fresh parsley, thinly-sliced lemon.

Heat oil in a wok, stir in celery ar onion. Cover and cook over a gent heat for 3 minutes.

Stir in garlic, mushrooms, chicke prawns, salt and pepper to taste.

Cover and continue cooking for 8-1 minutes, stirring occasionally. Stir lemon juice. Serve garnished wi parsley and lemon slices.
*To turn mushrooms: using a sm sharp knife make a series of curvir cuts about 5 mm apart, following t natural shape of the cap from the t of each cap to the base. Take out narrow strip along each indentation press firmly with the point of the knif

Serves 4.

STIR-FRY PORK and MUSHROOMS
in CIDER

30 ml oil.
175 g dwarf stick beans, cut into 5 cm lengths.
450 g pork fillet, cut into narrow strips.
1 large onion, cut into narrow, wedge-shaped strips.
350 g open cup mushrooms, wiped and sliced.
60 ml strong, medium-dry cider.
15 ml chopped, fresh sage.
12 pimento-stuffed olives.
Salt and pepper.
5-10 ml cornflour.

Heat oil in a wok, add beans, cover and cook for about 3 minutes. Add pork and onion and cook for 3 minutes.

Stir in mushrooms and cook a minute. Stir in cider, sage, olives and seasoning to taste. Cook for about 5 minutes.

Blend cornflour with a little water until smooth, then stir into pan. Bring to the boil, then serve.

Serves 4.

CHINESE VEGETABLE STIR-FRY (Illustrated)

30 ml sesame oil.
125 g baby corn cobs.
1 large red pepper, seeds removed and cut into narrow strips.
150 g mangetout, topped and tailed.
1 bunch spring onions, cut into 5 cm lengths.
275 g button mushrooms, wiped and halved.
2.5 cm fresh ginger, grated.
1 x 5 ml spoon ground ginger.
4 x 15 ml spoon soy sauce.
1 x 15 ml spoon set honey.
3 x 15 ml spoon tomato ketchup.
225 g fresh bean sprouts.
1 x 15 ml spoon cornflour.

Heat oil in a wok. Stir in baby corn, red pepper and mangetout. Cover and cook for 2 minutes.

Stir in spring onions and mushrooms and grated ginger, and cook another minute. Stir in ground ginger and cook a few seconds, then stir in soy sauce, honey and tomato ketchup.

Bring to the boil, cover, then cook gently for about 3 minutes. Stir in bean sprouts, and cook gently for 2 minutes.

Blend cornflour with a little water until smooth, then stir into the vegetables. Bring to the boil, then serve immediately.

Serves 4.

STIR-FRIED CHILLI BEEF with BEANS
(Illustrated)

575 g rump or sirloin steak, cut into thin strips.
Juice of 2 oranges made up to 250 ml with water.
1-2 dried red chillies, crushed.
2 x 15 ml spoon lemon juice.
30 ml oil.
1 large onion, sliced into wedges.
175 g broad beans.
1 red pepper, seeds removed and cut into thin strips.
300 g closed cup mushrooms, thickly sliced.
4 x 15 ml spoon peanut butter.
Salt and pepper.
To Garnish:
Chopped fresh herbs.

Place beef in a mixing bowl with orange juice and water, chillies and lemon juice. Mix well, cover and leave to marinate for at least 1 hour.

Drain beef from marinade, reserving juices. Heat oil in a wok and stir in beef and onion. Cover and cook for 3 minutes.

Stir in beans, red pepper and mushrooms. Cover and cook for 3 minutes.
Stir in reserved marinade. Bring to the boil, then stir in peanut butter and seasoning to taste.

Cook until sauce thickens. Garnish with fresh herbs.
Serves 4.

Continued from page 47

explosion. But it never came.

"Jolly good thing, too," he heard Peter Marchant say. "I've felt there should be something done about that mess for a long time, but of course, all that those money-conscious young fellows on the board are concerned about is the cash angle. I suppose they are right, in a sense, but I can't help feeling that —"

He bent closer to the window and stopped suddenly.

"Oh, hello, Russell. What are you doing down there?"

"He gets car-sick," Barbara put in nonchalantly, ignoring Russell's glare as he rose to his seat.

"Er, yes. Yes, that's right," he agreed, smiling sheepishly at Peter Marchant. "Helps, you know — travelling on the floor."

Marchant raised an eyebrow.

"I didn't know you were a friend of Barbara's," he said amiably. "Are you with her on this Brackley Head business, too?"

"No," Russell replied, but his voice was drowned out by Barbara.

"Yes," Russell agreed, a trifle dazed. "I am."

Marchant smiled benignly.

FIRST THINGS FIRST

The other day I went into my teenage son's bedroom for a clothes-hanger to air his shirt on. I was met by a scene of devastation.

His football kit was lying in a heap on the floor, his best shirt was crumpled on a chair, and trousers and his good jumper and socks were all in tangled piles.

I opened the wardrobe door and there, draped neatly over a hanger, were his two football scarves!

Just a question of priorities, I suppose!

"Good. Then as there are two of us who have some concern for the countryside, maybe we'll be able to get something done about it. Used to be a favourite place of mine in my young days. Went there a lot in the spring with Mary — my late wife. Lovely part of the country.

He smiled. "Still, sentiment's not really appreciated in business these days, is it?"

He laughed and patted the car. "Nice little buggy you've got there, Barbara," he said, then turned to Russell. "How about you and your young lady coming over for tea tomorrow. Say about four?"

Russell stared stupidly while Barbara made the appropriate arrangements.

Then just as they were about to say goodbye, Russell saw her —

his mother — hurrying down the road, obviously set on talking to Peter Marchant.

Oh, no, Russell thought, oh dear, no . . .

But his mother was alongside the car, and smiling happily.

"Well, Mrs Neilson," Peter Marchant said, returning her smile. "I've just been asking your son and his young lady to tea tomorrow. I wonder, would you like to come, too?"

Russell stared at them in disbelief. It isn't *really* happening, he told himself. Only it was — for his mother was accepting Marchant's invitation, and looking as if they were the best of friends!

"How can I refuse?" she said lightly. "Especially when you took all the trouble to come and talk to me about my letters."

She beamed triumphantly down at Russell.

"I'm just going shopping, Rusty," she said. "Be home soon."

She turned then and Peter Marchant fell into step with her. Together they walked off down the road.

RUSSELL stared dazedly after them.

"You see," Barbara said, turning to him. "He's not an ogre at all. In fact —" She laughed. "I think I've done you quite a bit of good there. Bet he never asked you to tea when he thought you were an old stuffed-shirt like the rest of them!"

She frowned at him for a moment. "You needn't worry about having to drag me along though. You can take your real 'young lady' and say I've come down with flu or something."

Russell had almost been on the point of laughing himself, a rare occurrence these days, but now his heart plummeted.

"Actually, I haven't got one, Barbara." He ran a finger lightly over her hand. "I don't suppose you'd feel like standing in for the day? I mean, after all, it was you he asked."

"Well, I suppose I might manage that," Barbara said cautiously.

Russell smiled. "I'll take you out to dinner tonight if you do."

She placed her hand in his. "You've got a deal, Mr Neilson. Only you must let me cook a meal for you one night next week," she added with mock formality. "Just to pay you back."

"And so on, for ever," he almost said, but decided it might be taking rather a lot for granted.

Instead he said, "I wonder if the daffodils will grow again after the place has been cleared." And immediately wondered why that had come into his head.

"We'll find out next spring," Barbara said, smiling. She eased her hand gently from his grip and returned it to the wheel of the car. "Now I suppose I'd better get you home, Russell."

"Rusty," he corrected.

He settled contentedly back into his seat. Yes, he was rather looking forward to next spring, all things considered. Though, come to think of it, the rest of the year could be quite promising too, now!

——————— * **THE END** * ———————

See Venice

Complete Story **By VERA PROCTOR**

and **Live**

Just a few short days of magic, but long enough to change an age-old saying.

"D ON'T be silly, Emma. It really is time you learned to put sense before sentiment," her father told her. Her mother, too, was practical.

"You mean well, dear," she said. "The holiday is a lovely idea, but Gran's sight is so poor that I doubt whether she'd appreciate the effort."

Emma sighed. "But it's *because* her sight is poor that I want to take her just now," she insisted. "By the end of the month she'll be in hospital, and if the operation doesn't go well . . ."

"It's a perfectly safe eye operation," her mother put in, "and she'll be quite all right afterwards."

Her mother glanced at the uncleared table, while her father gave his that's-the-end-of-the-matter look.

Emma opened her mouth, then closed it again. Why couldn't they understand, she fumed!

She turned to the door. For once, she decided, she could skip helping with the washing-up duty. For surely the idea she'd had concerning her grandmother was more important! Of course it was, she decided. Infinitely more important!

She hurried into the hall, picked up her coat and swiftly left the house.

Her grandmother lived in one of the one-roomed flats at Morton Old Folk's Home, near the centre of town, and as Emma hurried towards it, she wondered again how much longer the old lady would go on staying there.

After all, she'd always said it would be much better if her grandmother could move in with them — but, of course, her parents had had something to say about that, too.

In fact, it was only a few weeks ago that she'd last brought the subject up, she thought with annoyance.

"Mother is all right at the moment," her father had stated. "She knows there will be a room for her here later on, when she needs it."

"Why can't she have the room now — if not permanently, then for weekends and holidays?" Emma had asked.

But her mother had shaken her head. "No, Emma. You must understand that it really is better for elderly people to remain independent for as long as they possibly can."

Emma sighed now and hurried on. Twenty minutes later, she pushed open the front door of Morton House, smiled towards the two old people in the communal sitting-room, and hurried along the corridor.

She found her grandmother seated in an armchair drawn close to the radiator, staring towards the concrete square outside her window.

EMMA switched on the light and drew the curtains.

"Cold, Gran?" she asked, and plugged in the electric fire her grandmother was a little scared of using these days. "Shall I make us a cup of tea?"

Her grandmother relaxed and smiled gratefully as the extra warmth reached her. The old lady had her son's broad brow and firm chin, but there the resemblance ended. And she had a personality that was all her own— a carefree bubbling zest for life that Emma had always admired.

The old lady looked up at her now, and her smile broadened.

"There's a little of that sherry left, Emma," she whispered. "Shall we?"

"It's early for drinking, Gran." Emma returned the old lady's smile.

"Blow the time, if we feel like it!"

They giggled like schoolgirls, and Emma brought the bottle of sherry and placed a glass near her gran's fingers. "What'll we drink to, Gran?"

Immediately she wished she hadn't asked that, for it came to her that they should drink to the success of her grandmother's coming eye operation, and obviously the same thought came to the old lady, for her lips drooped a little.

"Gran," Emma said quickly, trying to cover her slip, "I've had an idea!"

"Have you now, lovey?" Emma's grandmother had a lilt in her voice — a sing-song note that was there because she had been born west of Swansea. She could spot a compatriot the world over, she'd said proudly once, no matter how carefully the lilt was disguised!

Now the old lady's eyes were wide, filled with interest.

Emma took a breath, then took the plunge.

"If you could have one wish, Gran, what would you like more than anything?" she asked, and even to her own ears it sounded so childish that she could almost hear her father saying, "Oh, child, do grow up!"

Her grandmother's pale fingers moved and rested on her arm. "You know what I'd like, lovey. It's back I'd like to go — back to Venice, once more."

"Tell me again about Venice," Emma said gently.

Her grandmother smiled happily. "Oh, I've told you. Ever since you were a little girl, I've told you. About the palaces and the gondolas. All silver . . . The waterways, a sheen of silver. Pale sun turning the beautiful buildings into silver after rain. Even the backs of the pigeons — pure silver.

"Your grandfather and I . . . on our honeymoon, of course . . . walked hand-in-hand and took it in turns to feed the pigeons. And, after rain, walking in the piazza was like gliding on a sheet of silver."

The old lady stopped and blinked.

"And you, Emma," she went on after a moment, "if you could have one wish?"

Emma laughed, a little embarrassed, as a secret thought came into her mind.

"You can tell me. Or maybe," her gran said, smiling, "I don't need to be told. As your father says, you're like me, Emma. And it doesn't matter a jot about this modern liberation business. You want what I always wanted."

"Romance?" Emma whispered.

"Romance that leads to love. You'll tell me, Emma, won't you, when you find a nice young man . . . But why haven't you found one . . . such a pretty girl!"

Emma shook her head, ruffling her hair. She'd often wondered if maybe her hair was too fine and pale. And her face? Was it chocolate-box pretty in an old-fashioned style, rather than in a bold, more modern way?

"I meet quite a few boys in the tourist agency, especially during lunch-hours," Emma admitted. "They come to ask questions and take away brochures. But they seem so . . . so sensible. Really they only come to pass their lunch-times, and in the end they go on holiday at ordinary times, to ordinary places."

Her grandmother thought about that for a moment, then asked, "And your idea?"

"I want us to have a holiday together," Emma said, then added quickly, "oh, I know we can't go far or for too long. But I thought, just for a long weekend, *soon* . . ."

"A holiday weekend before the end of the month?" her grandmother said a little shakily.

"That's it. I'll be able to make all the arrangements through the agency," Emma rushed on excitedly. "And we could fly! You'd be all right flying, wouldn't you, Gran, with me to look after you? You

Some Like It

THERE is a tendency to think that all plants do better in sunshine, but this is not so. There are lots of shrubs and flowering plants that prefer the shade and will not do their best elsewhere.

So if the sun never reaches some part of your garden because you happen to live on the wrong side of the street, or are shaded by tall trees, don't despair and don't try to grow particular types of plants simply because you like them.

There is nothing so sad as a plant that loves full sun just existing in a dull, shady place, when some other pretty thing would thrive there.

However unfriendly the situation, you should be able to find a few good-natured plants that will make a brave show. Give them plenty of encouragement to start with.

Make sure the ground is dug well and mix in whatever is available in

If your garden always seems to be in the shade don't despair — there are plenty of shy flowers and shrubs which really are happier out of the limelight!

the way of compost, manure, rotted leaves or peat. If your soil is clay add some sand or ashes as well.

A generous sprinkling of bonemeal will do nothing but good and last a long time.

Often a shady place is damp as well, but if the shade is caused by nearby trees, then thirsty roots may take all available moisture.

In this case don't leave plants and shrubs to take their chance, but water them frequently in dry weather and they will thank you for it.

By FLORENCE BASTIE

would like to go, wouldn't you, Gran?"

"Love to!" The old lady lifted her glass. "And where would we be going, lovey?"

"To Venice, of course, Gran. To *Venice.*"

INCREDIBLY, twelve days later they were there.

Yet it hadn't been easy organising everything. First they'd had to win over Emma's mother and father — who'd said they'd never get into a hotel in August anyway. Then there had been the actual arranging of it all — but Emma's office manager had helped there, and they'd been lucky to take over someone else's cancelled booking.

So in the end, Emma's mother and father had conceded and attended to practical things, like checking Gran's passport, and advising Emma how to act should her grandmother be taken ill, lose her papers, tablets or purse. Her father had also driven them to the airport.

COOL

STYRAX JAPONICA

The biggest headache is a completely sunless area under a north wall, but there are three wall shrubs that will relieve the gloom.

Cotoneaster horizontalis spreads its herring-bone branches attractively studded with red berries in autumn, while Pyracantha (Firethorn) has the added advantage of being evergreen as well as having berries of red, orange or yellow. Chaenomeles (Japonica) can be relied on to give a good display of scarlet or pink flowers in spring.

Few shrubs give more satisfactory results in a shady border beneath trees than the Partridge Berry, Leycesteria formosa.

It has white bell flowers surrounded with wine-coloured bracts from June to September followed by reddish-purple berries. It is not a spectacular shrub but it does well in town gardens and also in seaside districts. It grows to about five feet, and the flowers hang in ringlets which are sometimes known as "Granny's Curls."

The well-known Spiraea "Anthony Waterer" will grow well in shade, too, bearing long-lasting flat heads of crimson flowers. It is best cut down severely each spring.

Continued overleaf.

Now the flight to Venice was over and they were in a bus taking them towards the city.

"We'll soon be at the hotel," Emma said cheerily, for she'd noticed Gran was looking tired and frail. "You are all right, Gran?" she added, worried.

The old lady nodded. "Of course, lovey. It's wonderful."

But the bus only took them to the terminal in the city centre, and when they alighted, their surroundings didn't seem so very different from the bus terminal at home. Even the weather seemed the same. It was cold and drizzling.

How on earth would they set about finding their hotel, Emma wondered.

A package tour where you'd be looked after would be much more sensible, her mother's voice echoed in her mind.

She stood, dismayed by the wetness, trying desperately to recall the few Italian phrases she'd learned, while Gran pressed heavily on her

MOVING from shrubs to hardy plants, there is another spiraea-like perennial, Astilbe, also known as Goat's Beard. If, in addition to shade, the area is moist, Astilbes will revel in it.

Their crisply erect feathery plumes of pink, red or white flowers and delicately-cut foliage make them a glorious sight when in bloom June/August.

The elegant Japanese Anemone is another good subject for a shady border and in September is generous in producing white or mauvy-pink flowers.

Once these anemones get going there seems to be no stopping them. They spread like mad and I find mine popping up in stone steps and paved areas. I declared war on them, lost, and now they have the edge on me!

Lily of the Valley flourishes in the shade but it does need good rich soil to do really well. If starved, they drag themselves up all thin and wan looking.

Foxgloves are well known shade-fanciers and so is the Bleeding Heart, Dicentra, a fascinating plant with lacy leaves and arching stems hung with flowers like little pink lockets.

Gold is a most desirable colour in a shady spot, and Doronicums, or Leopard's Bane, make a bright splash. They grow about two foot high and bear large yellow daisy flowers very early in the year.

A pretty skirt for their slim stems is the blue cowslip, Pulmonaria, which forms neat round clumps of green leaves marbled with white and rosy flowers which gradually change to blue. Tuck in a few claret-coloured Primula Wandas and you've got a pleasing group.

Favourite plants in my damp and shady border are Hostas. I love them — and so do the slugs! If you ever decide to grow these Plantain Lilies mark the spot where you plant them, as they disappear below ground all winter, and then make a note to put down slug pellets the moment the little leaf spears show.

I grow two kinds, a slender-leaved one, H. fortunei aurea, all gold and green, and H. sieboldiana which produces masses of broad, heart-shaped leaves with a pleated effect, more blue than green in colour.

This latter one is popular with flower arrangers. There are several other kinds with leaves glossy or cream edged or banded down the centre with silvery white.

Another advantage of Hostas is that they grow densely and help smother weeds. ■

arm. And she never knew what she would have done next if it hadn't been for the stranger.

He came swinging along, smiling to himself; almost walked past, then stopped when he saw Emma's distress. He looked around 19, and was so good looking in a dark, Italian way that Emma could only stare into his velvet dark eyes, while he sang out in attractive pidgin-English: "*Mi scusi, signorina. I — help you?*"

At the sound of his voice Gran laughed suddenly and perked up.

"Yes, please," she accepted promptly, while Emma still hesitated.

"Look," said the boy, waving his arms as he led them to the waterway. "Gondola . . ." He frowned and shook his head. "Too mucha money. Take buso."

Gran chuckled again at his comic English, but Emma had never thought they'd be doing anything so ordinary as queueing by the jetty for a water bus, just as she did by a bus-stop at home!

She had to admit, too, that the bus journey itself was disappointing — just like any bus except it was moving on water instead of on a road. If the boy hadn't been there to query softly, "Tell me, please ... your name?" she would almost have felt like weeping.

"Emma Philips. And yours?"

"Antonio."

Antonio. Of course, that was just right!

"The Grand Canal!" Antonio announced later with a flourish, and then chatted about the buildings alongside. He took them right into their hotel and had a last, confidential word with Gran while Emma went to the desk.

She looked after him with regret as he waved and disappeared through the swing doors.

Later, when she and her grandmother had freshened up and were in the restaurant, Emma longed for Antonio to re-appear, for she couldn't understand the menu. Finally she ordered spaghetti bolognese, while Gran decided she couldn't manage that very well.

"Never mind," the old lady said cheerfully. "I'll have a nice sandwich."

But Emma couldn't share her grandmother's mood. She felt depressed at the way everything was turning out . . .

FOR breakfast next morning they were served only rolls and coffee, then they set out into a grey, cloudy Venice.

Glad to have found out about the water-buses, they boarded one that took them past some rather grim-looking buildings and on down the canal. After a time they got off and walked, wandering through little streets until they came to a square, where Gran suddenly stopped.

"I'd like to sit down now, dear," she said.

So they found a café and again Gran had a sandwich and coffee and Emma more spaghetti bolognese. But this time the spaghetti wasn't served as hot as it should have been, and Emma scarcely touched it. She felt a little lost and let down.

She turned to her grandmother, who was nibbling her way through her sandwich.

"How are you finding it all, Gran?" she asked, and she felt so low that her voice wobbled.

Her gran smiled. "Wonderful!" the old lady said, in a tone so sincere that Emma felt suddenly ashamed. She pulled aside a net curtain and peered out of the window, trying to discover why she herself wasn't finding Venice so wonderful.

As she looked, a grey mist came from nowhere and closed in. Emma shivered, and then she knew.

She was so very disappointed because . . . there was no silver anywhere! It wasn't at all like the Venice Gran had described so joyously. The huge buildings that flanked the Grand Canal had looked dingy and grey under a grey sky. And the paving-stones outside — they didn't glisten with silver, only with silly ordinary puddles! As for the pigeons . . . *nothing* could be greyer than the

Continued on page 69

THERE'S one good thing about the Women's Lib. movement — it's stopped me feeling guilty about not cleaning my house regularly.

After all, a week's supply of dust is as easy to wipe away as one day's supply. And because I realise that my kids won't be little for ever, I like to do things with them — like going swimming with Jane and taking Ricky to football matches.

But I *do* make an honest effort to clean my house whenever I can't find anything else to do.

At least, that's how things were until I got a letter from my cousin,

Marilyn — a whizz kid if ever I met one.

"I'll be passing through your town on a business trip," it said. "It's been years since we've seen each other, so I've decided to visit you. I'll arrive about four on Saturday.

"Love, Marilyn."

Now, Marilyn and I grew up together, as close as sisters until I married Bob and moved far away from home, so my first reaction was one of joy. My second reaction was one of horror.

How does Women's Lib. feel about entertaining relatives in a messy house?

Having A Right Old

Cleaning the house is one job I've never liked, says Roni Borden. But it was either that, or face getting the brush-off from my old school friend!

Bob and the kids consider it a bargain, having a happy mother instead of a tidy house. They don't even see the mess any more. But how would the flat look to an outsider?

And how would I feel if Marilyn tripped over something and broke her leg, or was so busy sneezing through clouds of dust she couldn't even talk to me?

I decided to discuss the matter with Bob.

"Where does comfortable living end and mess begin?" Bob wondered — he's an engineer and approaches things from a logical point of view.

"I don't think it's at dust on the table tops," he continued, drawing a design on the coffee table before he wiped the corner clean with his sleeve. "I don't even think that it's cobwebs hanging from the ceiling."

"No," I agreed. "They don't hang low enough to brush Marilyn's head, so I don't think they would bother her."

"I think the distinction between comfort and clutter is just a matter of degree," Bob went on. "It's all right to have the things you want out where you can use them, but if you have to lift your knee up to your chin to walk across the room, then that's mess."

I had to agree. Marilyn might not be fit enough for all the goose-stepping that was necessary to get around this house.

The letter from Marilyn had come on a Monday, giving me almost a week to get the place in order. By Saturday, I was sure, the place would look as neat as it had the first time my mother came to visit.

On Tuesday I looked around, trying to decide where to begin. But by the time I'd answered the phone, helped Ricky with his homework, and driven to the other side of town to pick up Jane, who was doing her homework with a friend, I had to hurry to get dinner ready on time.

After dinner our family relaxes and I wouldn't dream of disturbing everyone by doing housework after dinner . . .

SO the week went, and before I knew it, it was Saturday, and Marilyn would be here in the afternoon.

I was anxious to get started on the clean-up, but first I'd to get the children to and from their Saturday morning activities. By the time I finished my chauffeuring chores, it was lunchtime, and by the time we finished lunch I had about two hours to make the house "enter-able."

I rushed to begin the cleaning operation, starting by making our bed. To make the bed, I quickly pulled the sheets and blankets up, smoothing them out a little. Since I'd carefully put away our best bedspread after the last time I used it

E

(when my mother came to visit) I simply got it out of the cupboard and carefully threw it over the bed again.

Once the bed was done, I piled all the old newspapers on one side of the bed and stacked all the books and magazines on the other.

I know Marilyn wouldn't object to this kind of clutter because she and I have always been somewhat bookish, and this would prove to her that just because a woman gets married and has children, she doesn't automatically stop thinking.

My last job in the bedroom was to kick all the dirty clothes under the bed — at least they'd be in a safe place till wash-day.

Time taken: twenty-two minutes.

The bathroom was my next target. I wiped off the mirror and the counter top with the flannel and dried it with the towel. I also cleaned the corners of the floor with the towel, being particularly careful to wipe behind the door.

Then I hid both the flannel and the towel behind the door of the shower. I put some clean towels out, put a fresh roll of toilet paper into the holder and left the room with a smug feeling of satisfaction.

Time taken: eighteen minutes.

The living-room was easy.

First I picked up all the toys and dumped them into the children's toy box. Next I picked up the newspapers and magazines and added them to the pile in my bedroom. Then I picked up the dirty clothes and threw them under my bed. Everything left over went into the bin.

Time taken: nineteen minutes.

Next, I toyed with the idea of cleaning, or at least organising, the children's room, but decided it would take less time if I pulled the door shut and pencilled a "Do Not Disturb" sign on the outside.

Time taken: seven minutes.

The kitchen's probably the most complex room to do, but, I reasoned, no-one expects it to be too clean — a sterile-looking kitchen is a sure sign of a family that eats baked beans all the time.

I really did feel, though, that I should wash the dirty dishes and pots. It's not a fun job, but for sanitary reasons it seemed like the thing to do.

Next, I cleared the worktops by stuffing everything I could into the cabinets. I realised that I would probably never find any of those things again, but no matter. Seeing Marilyn again was worth it.

Unfortunately, not everything would fit into the cabinets, so I arranged the leftovers — the mixing bowl, two forks, an egg beater, three pot covers and a pot holder — into an artistic pile. Then I wiped up all the glaring spots on the kitchen floor.

Time taken: twenty minutes.

To complete the whole job, I hurried from one piece of furniture to another with a giant duster.

Time taken: sixteen minutes.

As a final test, I stood in the doorway of each room and glanced in quickly — most people only glance into rooms.

Time taken: four minutes.

Total time taken: one hour, fifty-five minutes.

That left me five minutes to get washed and into some decent clothes. I hurried, and just as I finished pulling on my sweater, I heard the front door open. Marilyn was here! I ran to the door with outstretched arms.

"Marilyn. How marvellous to see you!"

We had a wonderful visit that afternoon, reminiscing about our childhood and catching up on the latest gossip.

As she was about to leave, Marilyn suddenly turned to me.

"I love your house," she said. "It has that comfortable, lived-in look." ∎

"I MUST REMEMBER NOT TO FORGET TO REMEMBER..."

Poetry is a wonderful thing, says SHEILA BYRNE. Treat it right and it can give you a fantastic memory. . .

SOME people pride themselves on never forgetting a name. Others never forget a face. I remember neither.

Most women find a shopping list a helpful aid to memory. I always made a careful list, too — but forgot to bring it with me.

My family got quite used to me pouring out water from the teapot because I'd forgotten to put in the tea. I invariably omitted the sugar from stewed fruit and even the ginger from what was meant to be a ginger cake.

I visited the Lost Property Office almost daily in my efforts to locate parcels, umbrellas, gloves, bags and library books. The very nice man there suggested I should leave my entire wardrobe with him and just call for things as I needed them.

The climax came, though, when I put away the money for the poll tax last year. I haven't remembered where, from that day to this.

"Things have really gone too far this time," I decided. "I'll have to do something about myself before I forget who I am."

I mentioned my problem to an amateur psychologist of my acquaintance. He told me there was quite a simple way out of my dilemma.

"Turn your thoughts into rhyme," he said. "It's a certain way to remember."

"Suppose you'd put the poll tax on top of the kitchen cabinet? You'd just invent a rhyme when you were doing it — something like this:

I've put it on top of the kitchen cabiNET,
I'll always remember, I'll never never forGET.

He seemed extraordinarily proud of achieving this jingle. He went on to suggest I should concentrate on places that might rhyme more easily, because it was unlikely I would have his gift for scansion.

NEXT morning before setting off for the shops, I tried out the idea in the hall.

Eeeny-meeny, miney mo,
For eggs and rhubarb I must go.

All the way to the shops I muttered it under my breath. It worked like a charm. I could hardly wait for the next day.

This time I had a longer list, so I tried alliteration.

Mustard, marmalade and mincemeat, macaroni, margarine,
Mallow, mandarins and matches (Memo, don't forget the cream).
Potatoes, porridge, pickles, plaice, parsley and white paint (My memory's getting good already, blow me if it ain't!)
Stamps and sauce and sewing thread, salmon, sago, soap.
Soup and sweets and sausages (Could I forget them? Nope).

AFTER a while, of course, I got rather weary of inventing. "Why not make use of poems I know well?" I asked myself.

I started with the easiest one I knew. No doubt you'll recognise it.

Water, water everywhere and not a drop to drink.
A tin of peas, a loaf of bread, a stopper for the sink."

I went on to better things. All the poems of my schooldays, I found,

could easily be utilised.

When I have fears that I may cease to be,
Before my pen has gleaned my teeming brain,
Remember raisins, currants and some tea,
And fluid to clean the outside drain.

There was one big snag in this method. I found that although I no longer needed to mutter it all the way to the shops, I had to repeat the first line before I got to the list of goods.

The day I was working on, *Wee, sleekit, cow'ring, tim'rous beastie,* (I wanted a bag of flour, an ounce of yeast-ie) the shopman looked at me so peculiarly that I quite lost the thread of the thing and slunk off home — minus my shopping.

I've overcome all these minor difficulties now, though. I use popular songs so nobody thinks it odd if I hum a line or two in a shop.

Moonlight and roses, bring wonderful memories of you,
Two pounds of apples, a large tin of Irish stew.

And how do I remember names? Ah! There you have me. I did try very hard with these but my neighbours and acquaintances are blessed with names like Fitzmaurice, Tumulty and Peavoy and who could possibly think up rhymes for those? Next time I move house, I'll make sure my neighbours have names like Glynn *(It would be a sin to forget Mrs Glynn)* or Brown *(Every time I go to town, I'm sure to meet with Mrs Brown).*

Meantime I just smile at everyone I meet. It has worked well.

In fact, Mrs I-forget-her-name told me the other day that I was known all over the neighbourhood as "that nice, friendly woman who lives up the road."

Evidently no-one can remember my name either. ∎

Continued from page 63
pigeons! There was no silver anywhere . . .

"What's the time, lovey?" Gran said suddenly.

Emma glanced at her wrist-watch. "Just turned two," she said, then added despondently, "What would you like to do next, Gran?"

With an eagerness that was disconcerting, the old lady said, "Let's make our way back to the hotel. Perhaps we could get a pot of tea there, and I could put my feet up for a bit."

So they left the café and caught the water-bus back to the hotel. But as they entered, Emma's heart leapt as she saw the dark, handsome young man sitting in the foyer.

"Antonio!" she exclaimed, and Gran smiled broadly, her tiredness dropping away.

Antonio swung round and grinned at them, then he stood up and came across.

"Point me towards the lounge and I'll order tea for myelf," sang out Gran happily. "And perhaps this young man will show you a few more sights, Emma."

But as Antonio hurried forward to find Gran a seat, Emma heard herself saying, as her mother might have done, "Go out with a strange young man, in a strange city?"

Then she blinked and found her grandmother smiling at her.

"He's a charming young man, Emma," the old lady declared, as if she had known Antonio all her life. "Now off you go and enjoy yourself!"

With that, Antonio came over to take her arm, and they swung outside together. And, for the first time, Emma began to feel excited about being in Venice.

Antonio handed her into a gondola and they passed the same buildings, the same churches and palaces, and came eventually to the same square with the big wet paving stones.

There was the same café, and the pigeons. Emma had more spaghetti, shared some wine, went dancing, and stayed out so late that when she at last hurtled into the hotel and up to her room she felt ashamed.

"Oh, Gran," she burst out. "I'm sorry to have left you alone so long . . ."

The old lady smiled and shook her head. "Not at all, lovey, I've been happy enough," she said, then added gently, "Have you, Emma?"

"Oh, Gran, you've no idea!" Emma twirled until her fine pale hair sprang around her face and covered her blushes. "And . . . do you know . . ." she breathed.

"What, lovey?"

"Everything *is* silver! The churches and the buildings . . . everything! The mist lifted and the sun came out, just for a little, and such a pale sun. But it was wonderful. Beautiful! Silver everywhere — glinting from the palaces, the water, the sky. Even from the pigeons!"

"Why, of course," her grandmother said, surprised. "I told you that, didn't I?"

NEXT morning, Antonio came for them and they all went to church. It was a different Antonio Emma saw then, a young man who seemed as uncertain of the ritual as she was, but who appeared to be giving thanks, with quiet sincerity and without embarrassment, in his own way.

And then it was time to go back to the hotel, so that Emma and her grandmother could have lunch before catching their flight back to England.

The three of them stood in the foyer, Emma holding her breath in anticipation, waiting for Antonio to enthuse in his funny English about the good time they'd had, maybe even to throw his arms around her in sorrow at parting, and to make fervent promises to keep in touch.

But Antonio still seemed strangely bemused, and simply clasped her hands in his and said, *"Arrivederci. Arrivederci."* Then he was gone.

Emma walked into the restaurant with tears filling her eyes. She knew now that all she'd heard about Italian boys was true. They simply amused themselves with girl tourists, had fun where they could, and then . . . waited for the next one to come along.

TIRED, Gran?" Emma asked, when they were at last settled into their plane seats. Neither of them had spoken much on the journey out to the airport. And even now Emma still felt terribly depressed. Gran was apparently lost in her memories.

"I'm thirsty I am, if that's anything," Gran's voice lilted out.

"I'll get the hostess as soon as we get airborne," Emma promised, and she was leaning over to fasten her grandmother's seat-belt when Gran stayed her hand.

Emma glanced at her. The old lady seemed to be listening for

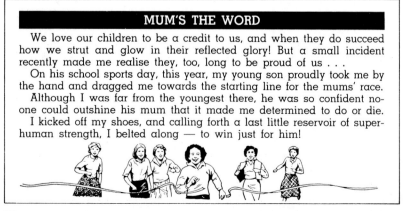

MUM'S THE WORD

We love our children to be a credit to us, and when they do succeed how we strut and glow in their reflected glory! But a small incident recently made me realise they, too, long to be proud of us . . .

On his school sports day, this year, my young son proudly took me by the hand and dragged me towards the starting line for the mums' race.

Although I was far from the youngest there, he was so confident no-one could outshine his mum that it made me determined to do or die.

I kicked off my shoes, and calling forth a last little reservoir of super-human strength, I belted along — to win just for him!

something.

"What is it, Gran?"

But her gran simply smiled and shook her head without answering, and Emma jumped, startled, when a male voice, full of quiet merriment, said quietly into her ear, "Happy, are you, then?"

Emma swung round to look straight into mischievous eyes.

She stared with astonishment at the young man standing in the aisle. "Antonio! What are you doing here?"

"Going back." He grinned. "Going home."

"What!"

His grin widened. "I had a week owing to me. Venice was the long-saved-for holiday, but rather a lonely holiday — until the last few days."

Emma frowned, bewildered. His comic accent had gone, and quite suddenly Antonio didn't look Italian at all.

"But you're . . . you're *English*, Antonio!"

"Tony, not Antonio. But I am *not* English!" He sounded outraged.

"Born in the Rhondda Valley, or not far from it, I shouldn't wonder." Gran chuckled.

He smiled and nodded. " Tony Price is my real name and it's true I was born in the Rhondda."

He turned and looked at Emma. "And I'm sorry about the deception, but if you'd only known how bored I was before you showed up.

"I — I wasn't sure if you'd look at me twice if I'd admitted I was just an ordinary garage mechanic. And, besides, I really did want to practise my Italian. I've been going to night classes and . . ."

His voice petered out and he smiled, a little shamefaced.

"I'm sorry, Emma," he ended. "It was silly."

"Sorry?" Emma looked at him in wonder. "But your Italian was marvellous." Suddenly she felt like the happiest girl in the world.

"Where are you sitting, Tony, lad?" her grandmother put in.

"At the back." He smiled at Emma. "I've got three seats all to myself."

"Well, I should just like to sit and be quiet and close my eyes," Gran said, and all at once the old lady did look quite frail and very tired.

"But have you enjoyed it, Gran?" Emma urged once more.

Her grandmother opened her eyes. And those eyes seemed to have lost their opaqueness and appeared very blue, and very young now.

And her smile was beautiful, too, as she sang out, "I've had a wonderful trip, thank you, lovey. Shall never forget it. Now off you go with Tony . . ."

Emma went. She ordered tea for Gran, then she went along to the back seat. And she, too, had a wonderful trip. Both she and Tony, had a wonderful time talking and making plans as only two people who hope to see a lot more of each other can . . .

——————— * **THE END** * ———————

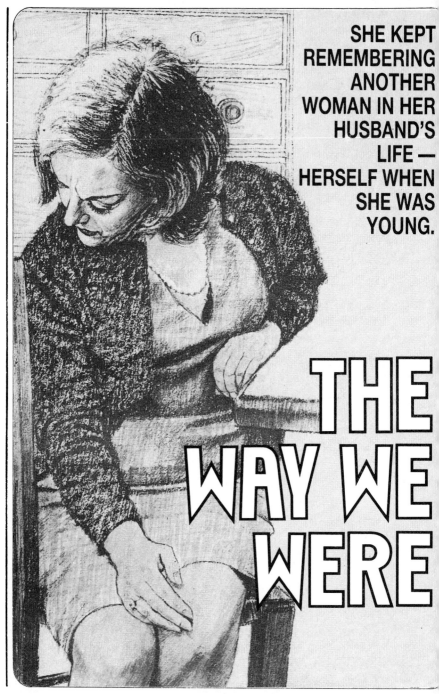

SHE KEPT
REMEMBERING
ANOTHER
WOMAN IN HER
HUSBAND'S
LIFE —
HERSELF WHEN
SHE WAS
YOUNG.

THE WAY WE WERE

CLARE WATKINS examined her freshly-manicured nails and tightened the clasp on the tiny gold wristwatch. Ten minutes and the taxi would be there, she thought, taking a deep breath in an effort to relieve the suffocating tightness in her chest.

What do other wives do in this situation, she wondered yet again, as she peered critically at her reflection — a demoralising ritual she had come to perform increasingly since finding the discarded letter in Alan's pocket.

What had made Alan, a loving husband, suddenly decide he needed more from life than a devoted wife, a beautiful home and a successful career?

How long had there been this — this crack in her marriage? And how long might it have gone on, slowly widening without her knowing, if she hadn't found that letter intended for another woman?

Tracing a finger along the taxi window, she wondered, with a feeling approaching panic, what this other woman was like. Very young? Beautiful?

The other woman! The hateful words hammered round in her brain as she pressed her palms to her cheeks, willing herself to remain calm. It was like one of those television plays, she thought.

She must pull herself together, she knew, and decide what to do. But how could she? It was like groping in the dark.

All she knew was that her name was Rosemary, that she was an artist and that she in some way had shown Alan a facet of life that had made him dissatisfied with the one he'd carved out for himself.

Clare stared absently out of the taxi window, her mind going again to the crumpled sheet of paper she'd found. The words had been imprinted in her mind as again and again she had gone over them, trying in vain to find the answer to her questions, while conjuring up a picture of the girl, or woman, for whom the letter had been written.

COMPLETE STORY By JANET HARTSHORNE

Usually, Clare imagined her to be a young, golden girl in full bloom of youth, making her all the more conscious of the lines that had appeared around her own eyes . . .

My Dear Rosemary, the letter had begun. *When I first came to your studio I had no way of knowing the effect it would have on my life. Perhaps if I had, I would never have come.*

In your own special way you manage to inject some of your own vibrant joy of living, not only into your pictures, but into others, too. For me, walking into your studio is like walking into sunshine, and the rest of the world seems that much greyer than before.

You can never know how hard it is for me to write this letter — and say that I won't be coming back. You see, Rosemary, however grey the world I live in is, I'm too much a part of it now, and it of me to —

Here the letter had ended abruptly, and a deeply-etched line had been struck through it before it had been crumpled into a ball and left, forgotten, in the pocket of his jacket.

Had that vicious line through the words been a sudden, defiant refusal to turn his back on Rosemary and all she stood for, Clare had wondered desperately when the first horror had left her, or had he rewritten the letter and sent it?

"WHICH house, dear?" The taxi driver's sudden query startled Clare out of her helpless jumble of thoughts.

"Drop me off at the corner, please," she told him as he pulled into Queen's Road, feeling the need to walk for a few minutes in the open air to steady her nerves.

It took only a few more minutes to walk to the address she wanted down the long, tree-lined road with its large Georgian houses on one side, and a vast expanse of parkland on the other.

Initially she'd felt disgust at the underhand way she had searched through Alan's pockets to find his diary. But then the feeling had given way to one of hurt and anger at the injustice of the situation that had forced her to do such a thing.

Scribbled at the back of the well-thumbed book, she had found what she was looking for.

Rosemary, 17 Queen's Road.

Suddenly, as she neared number 17, Clare remembered the painting Alan had given her for her last birthday, and wondered why she hadn't thought of it before.

It was of a little girl, so wonderfully alive as she ran through a meadow, primroses clutched in her hand. She had almost felt the warmth of the sun on her own skin and smelt the delicate flowers just by looking at it.

She recalled her admiration for the artist who could transmit such feeling on to canvas. But then she had known nothing of Rosemary.

Standing at the door of number 17, Clare rang the bell and wondered brokenly how many times Alan had stood here, waiting to escape from the greyness of his world . . .

She stared at the smock-clad figure who opened the door.

"I . . . I'd like to see some paintings," she stumbled.

She had been prepared to hate the golden girl of her imagination and was caught unawares by the pleasant woman inviting her in, for she could find nothing she could hate in the spontaneous friendliness she offered.

"Wander round and if there's anything you like, I'll tell you the worst," Rosemary invited her, as they entered the bright, airy room which served as her studio.

The autumn sun that shone through the large windows merely added to the riot of colour everywhere. Several half-finished pictures stood leaning against the walls, together with dozens of completed ones, every one of them breathing life, just as the little girl in the painting at home did.

"Coffee?" Rosemary asked, pouring it out without waiting for a reply.

Clare followed Rosemary as she walked round the studio, pointing out first one picture and then another. Frequently, she set her drink down to use her expressive hands to demonstrate a point, and Clare found herself unwittingly caught up in her vivacious enthusiasm.

Watching Rosemary as she ran fingers through her hair falling in soft disorder about her face, Clare could see that no-one could remain immune to the woman's magnetism. Rosemary was probably only a year or two younger than herself and yet there was the sparkle of youth about her which would never be stifled by day-to-day living. The whole business of living was obviously some great adventure to be enjoyed and shared, and Clare envied her.

THE smell of oil paint and turpentine, the paint-splattered coffee mugs and the half-finished work, all combined to remind her of another time. The time she and Alan had turned their spare bedroom into an impromptu studio. And, somehow, it wasn't the well-groomed, successful Alan she pictured here, escaping for a while from the irksome necessities of a well-regulated life, but a young, struggling, enthusiastic Alan. Suddenly, Clare knew that this was how he must feel when he came to this place.

What had he lost along the road to success, she wondered. What had they *both* lost? And surely if they could both have this same feeling, here in this studio, it wasn't too late to find it again together . . .

As though sensing her desire to be alone, Rosemary returned to her work, leaving Clare to wander round the collection of paintings undisturbed.

A swirling mass of colour depicting a group of dancers caught her eye. She could almost feel the beat of the music and hear the swish of their skirts, as she moved forward to study it more closely.

Her heart gave a lurch as she saw the painting standing behind it. Familiar grey eyes surveyed her from the canvas and her hands trembled as she bent to pick it up.

"I'm afraid that one isn't for sale."

Rosemary's voice was soft over her shoulder and Clare turned, almost afraid of what she would read in her face. But Rosemary's expression, though thoughtful, told her nothing.

"I never really finished that one," she said, taking the painting from her.

It looks finished, Clare thought, her gaze held by the portrait, so vivid, so alive that she almost expected it to move. The hair with its touch of grey at the temples was exactly right, as were the gentle grey eyes. It was a perfect likeness of Alan and yet it wasn't.

Suddenly, she knew why. The touch of grey in his hair, the

network of tiny lines surrounding his eyes were there, yes, but the laughter lurking in his eyes and the alert enthusiasm for life just below the surface, they were the Alan of another time. A young, carefree Alan she hadn't seen for so long . . .

"Did he sit for you?" she asked Rosemary.

"No. He often used to come and browse round and gradually I stored enough details in my mind to paint it from memory."

"I would love to buy it."

Rosemary frowned. "Why?"

Keeping her eyes on the portrait, Clare avoided her gaze.

"He — he looks like someone I used to know a long time ago."

Shaking her head, Rosemary replaced the canvas. "I'm sorry."

Clare couldn't begin to understand the other woman's feelings, why she had painted the portrait, and why she refused to sell it . . . Had she loved Alan, or had theirs simply been a bond of understanding between two sensitive people?

TROUBLE AFOOT

I recently bought a pair of summer sandals with dark, blue-flowered denim straps.

I wore them on the first hot day and was quite pleased with them — until I took them off! That's when I found that my tights and toes had turned blue.

I took them back to the shop and, after explaining what had happened, the manager said:

"You haven't been wearing them in this hot weather, have you?"

Next year, I'll save my summer sandals for the first snowfall!

She looked up. A bowl of marigolds on the window-sill in front of her reminded Clare of her own elegant flower arrangement at home, its colours blending with the tasteful décor of the lounge. Yet why did this untidy mass of flowers breathe so much more life into the room than her carefully-arranged ones?

Maybe that was it, Clare thought. It was more than just the flowers, perhaps their whole life was too carefully arranged.

HER mind went to the unused canvases and paints at home in the attic, and she remembered how, in the early days, they would take picnics down to the river and spend hours trying to capture some of it. And how they would return home, tired and content, their arms full of wild flowers and paints and half-finished pictures.

But, gradually, the paints had been put away with the incomplete pictures — and a few forgotten dreams.

Clare thought of those very early days when they had first moved into their house. After they'd bought a few essential items of furniture they had spent the remainder of their money on an expensive carpet for the large lounge. And, as they'd admired the vast room, adorned with nothing but the rich deep-pile carpet, they'd vowed that this was only the beginning.

They had thrown more parties than they had ever done since, Clare remembered. Everyone had sat around on the rich carpet or on cushions, eating cheese and sausages and drinking cider.

And on Sundays, Alan would strum his guitar and they'd laugh and sing and make their plans, leaving the outside world to take care of itself.

Their first baby, Louise, had come along a couple of years later, but she hadn't been followed by the other children they had hoped for. Alan had climbed the ladder of success with unexpected speed, becoming chief partner in a reputable firm of solicitors before he was 35, and one child hadn't been a drain on their resources that the big family they'd hoped for would have been. Perhaps life had been too easy for them.

They had been hard-up, it was true, but only while they were young enough for it to be fun. Soon the rich carpet was accompanied by all the other symbols of a very comfortable home and the days of cider parties were over. Even the once-loved guitar had joined the discarded canvases in the attic.

Now a good sherry and delicate savouries, taken with stiff solicitors and their wives, amidst polite conversation, was the order of the day, and Clare had believed that this was all they wanted . . . while somewhere, deep within them both, remained two people who, once in a while, needed to escape to the river bank and be themselves.

I'D like to buy this one," Clare announced as she spotted a picture of a stretch of sun-dappled water, fringed by rushes whispering in the breeze.

It might have been an omen, she thought, as she left Rosemary and made her way back down the tree-lined road, with the hap-hazardly-wrapped parcel under her arm. An omen telling her to stop sometimes and remember the important things — the "fun" things.

Suddenly, she found herself making plans. Now that Louise was away at college the weekends seemed far too quiet. It was near winter now, she knew, but when the sun shone this autumn, they would take a picnic to their old haunt again.

She stopped and gazed into a grocer's window. Then, quickly she marched in and bought cheese, and sausage, and cider.

And later, as she let herself into the deserted house, Clare realised just how hungry she was. She had been unable to think of eating anything before going to visit Rosemary, but now she felt happier, somehow optimistic, about the future.

It was as though she had been given a new lease of life, she thought, as she prepared a quick meal for herself.

Afterwards she automatically began to start washing the dishes she had used, then stopped herself.

A picture of Rosemary flashed before her, dumping the coffee mugs into the sink along with the jar of paint brushes, before returning to the painting she was working on, and deliberately Clare set her dishes down. They could wait . . .

IT was only when Clare heard Alan calling anxiously up the stairs that she realised how late it was, how wrapped up she'd been in what she was doing . . .

Pushing back the scarf round her hair with a dusty hand, she peered down through the attic trapdoor and met her husband's bewildered stare.

"What on earth are you doing up there?" he asked. "I thought you were ill when I saw the dirty dishes and no sign of dinner."

"Never mind the dishes," Clare told him. "Here, take these from me." She handed him down a heap of canvases, together with a very dusty box of oil paints.

"What . . ." he began ". . . what about dinner?"

Clare passed down a handful of brushes and a palette.

"You and I are going to have a go at painting again," she said briskly, wiping her face with the back of her hand, "and dinner can wait. We'll have something in a minute or two and I'll cook later. It's time we got down to the business of enjoying life again."

She saw him stiffen and colour slightly as he avoided her eyes.

"How did you know?" he asked, without looking up.

Climbing down to stand beside him, she brushed the dust from her hands.

"Does it matter, at the moment?"

Suddenly, he looked very sad. "Clare, I . . . I don't know what to say," he began, sighing.

"Then don't," she said, slipping her arm through his. "Come on, let's go downstairs and have a long cool glass of cider."

"Cider?" Alan frowned. "What's wrong with a glass of sherry?"

"We've had too many glasses of sherry on too many evenings, that's what's wrong. Go and put something comfortable on and we'll look through some of these old works of art and see how bad we really were."

"Aren't you going to wash your face first?"

He grinned, looking very much like Rosemary's portrait of him, Clare realised, swallowing to ease the sudden ache in her throat.

"No!" she said. "Bring your guitar when you come down, it's leaning against the wall behind you."

"You do realise," Alan said, idly strumming the dusty strings, "that you're quite mad!"

"That is one of the nicest things you could have said to me."

She smiled. "The other would be that you still . . ."

"That I still love you?" he asked.

Clare nodded.

"I always have," he told her, putting the guitar down and pulling her to him. "But maybe, for a time, I forgot just how much."

——————— * **THE END** * ———————

78

It's not what you say (But the way that you say it)

So you think you know your way around? Lesley Crosland helps us read between the lines . . .

——— RESTAURANTS AND MENUS ———

The Wording . . .	The Meaning . . .
"Smothered in French brandy"	The merest trickle of cheap cooking brandy has been added.
"Caressed in a cream and brandy sauce"	Swimming in a thick, calorie-ridden, sickly concoction.
"Rolls, warm from our ovens"	A quick burst in the microwave and you can be conned.
"Nouvelle cuisine"	You don't get much — be prepared to leave hungry.
"Our seasonal special dish"	They've managed to get hold of a job lot cheaply and they need to get it sold fast.

——— ESTATE AGENTS ———

Their Description . . .	True Picture . . .
"Ripe for development."	"A dump."
"Homely."	"Messy."
"Manageable garden."	"Can't get a deck-chair in it."

"Cosy."	"Too small to swing a cat."
"Conveniently situated for station."	"The track runs right next to your house, and trains thunder past all hours of the day and night."
"Tastefully decorated to a high standard."	"Fourteen layers of floral wallpaper will have to come off."
"Cottage-style kitchen."	"An unfitted disaster area, with some sink dating from the turn of the century."
"Designed with small windows for energy conservation."	"Dark and depressing with small panes set high up."
"At a realistic price."	"You're going to have to spend £20,000 on it to make it habitable."
"Tucked away in a cul-de-sac."	"Crammed in, with no space."
"Surprisingly spacious."	"It looks minute from the outside."

─────────────── **YOUR SPOUSE** ───────────────

What He Says . . .
"You look well."

(After a new recipe)
"That was different."

"That dress is nice."

"You don't need to go on a diet."

What He Means . . .
"You look fat."

"Don't bother again, I'd rather have steak and chips."

"It's a nice dress — but on someone else."

"I'm not eating salad every night for a month, just to keep you company."

What She Says . . .
"We've been married ten years next Thursday."

"I really love fresh flowers."

"Look, I don't want a row."

"Do you fancy cooking tonight?"

What She Means . . .
"Take me out for a romantic dinner for two."

"Why do you never buy me any?"

"But you're definitely in the wrong, so you'd better apologise straight-away!"

"Either you take me out for a meal, go and get a take-away — or we don't eat!" ■

Dainty Detail

You can transform a plain blouse with this delicate embroidery — and it's easy, too!

Instructions and diagrams overleaf

Continued from previous page

Dainty Detail

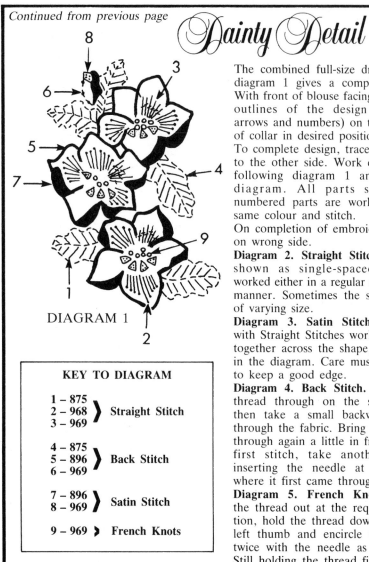

DIAGRAM 1

KEY TO DIAGRAM

1 – 875
2 – 968 } **Straight Stitch**
3 – 969

4 – 875
5 – 896 } **Back Stitch**
6 – 969

7 – 896
8 – 969 } **Satin Stitch**

9 – 969 } **French Knots**

Materials — Of **Anchor Stranded Cotton:** 1 skein each Winter Green 875, Dusky Pink 896, Strawberry 968 and 969. Use 2 strands throughout. Ladies' blouse similar to that shown. **Milward International Range crewel needle No. 8.**

The combined full-size drawing and diagram 1 gives a complete motif. With front of blouse facing, trace the outlines of the design (omitting arrows and numbers) on to one side of collar in desired position.

To complete design, trace in reverse to the other side. Work embroidery following diagram 1 and key to diagram. All parts similar to numbered parts are worked in the same colour and stitch.

On completion of embroidery, press on wrong side.

Diagram 2. Straight Stitch. This is shown as single-spaced stitches worked either in a regular or irregular manner. Sometimes the stitches are of varying size.

Diagram 3. Satin Stitch. Proceed with Straight Stitches worked closely together across the shape, as shown in the diagram. Care must be taken to keep a good edge.

Diagram 4. Back Stitch. Bring the thread through on the stitch line, then take a small backward stitch through the fabric. Bring the needle through again a little in front of the first stitch, take another stitch, inserting the needle at the point where it first came through.

Diagram 5. French Knots. Bring the thread out at the required position, hold the thread down with the left thumb and encircle the thread twice with the needle as in Fig. 1. Still holding the thread firmly, twist the needle back to the starting point and insert it close to where the thread first emerged (see arrow). Pull thread through to the back and secure for a single French Knot or pass on to the position of the next stitch as in Fig. 2.

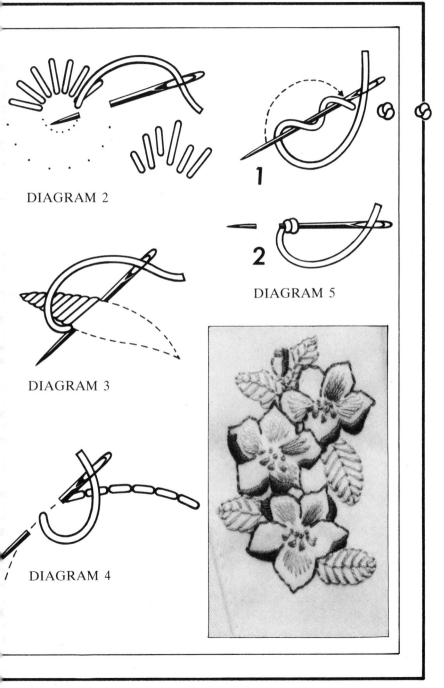

DIAGRAM 2

DIAGRAM 3

DIAGRAM 4

1

2

DIAGRAM 5

M^{Y} mother will be waiting for me.

Our home is only 10 minutes from the station, and although every time I tell her I can easily walk, she always comes.

I phone home once a week, but still the moment she sees me she asks a list of questions. Am I eating enough? Have I remembered to take my vitamin pills?

She tells me, each time, too, that I'm too thin, and that I must make sure to get at least one early night a week.

I don't mind this, and I laugh, as I look down at my mother. She's half a head shorter now than I am, but slim and brown. Her hair has highlights where the first grey is coming.

FAMILY TIES

She had made up her mind to break them. But to do so she had to make one last journey home.

I don't mind it, but — because of the way she is, because she is my mother, because there is a deep and abiding love between us — I wonder how I am going to tell her.

For how can you tell your mother something that is going to take the warm and loving laughter out of her eyes?

It would be easier, somehow, if I was coming home to tell her I was pregnant. She would be shaken and distressed, but — she would know

Complete Story By
ALISON REDFORD

what to do. She would take me in her arms, and we would cry together. We would talk about telling my father and about the things that must be done and decided.

But instead, I have come home to tell my mother and father that I am going to live with Rick.

Somehow I am going to try to make them see that for Rick and me, love is too precious to be bound in a wedding ring and too individual to be lost in marriage.

Love, for Rick and me, has to be free.

We could be like so many other people I know and just keep quiet, say nothing to my folk. There's his place and there is the arrangement Kay and Sally and I have that each one of us has the flat to ourselves one evening a week.

But Rick and I, we don't want any hole-in-the-corner stuff. We want our love to be honest and open. And we want to be together.

It's almost a month now since Rick asked me if I would move in with him.

I told him I couldn't start living with him until I told my mother and father what I was going to do. He has been very patient. He laughs at

me, a warm, loving laugh, because I am old fashioned, and he kisses me.

The train draws in, and my mother is waiting for me.

The old dog is beside her, and in spite of all that is weighing so heavily on me, my heart lifts as the dog's stump of a tail wags furiously. For he. is 12, and each time I go away from home I wonder if he will be there to meet me next time.

I have to greet him before my mother and I can hug each other, for he is whining with pleasure, his old eyes suddenly bright and clear again as he realises that it really is me.

"Shep, you're the stupidest dog I've ever known," I tell him fondly.

My mother and I laugh at him, and then she looks up at me.

"I know," I tell her, still smiling. "I'm too thin, and I haven't had enough early nights."

"Just as long as we've got that clear," she replies comfortably and takes my old duffel-bag.

I lift the small suitcase and we leave the station.

"Shall we have a coffee at The Copper Kettle on the way home?" she asks.

I shake my head.

"I'd rather go on home," I tell her.

I want to get this over, I want the air clear between us, I want this brought into the open.

"Yes, perhaps we'd better go home," she agrees. "I did promise Beth we'd go over some time this morning because she takes the baby to the clinic in the afternoon, so we might miss them. And since you're only staying until tomorrow afternoon, there isn't much time."

Her voice is calm and matter-of-fact, yet I feel warm colour flood my cheeks. I haven't been home for three weeks, and — after today — I don't quite know when I'll be back again.

"How is Timmy?" I ask, and I think that I don't really want to see my sister, Beth. I'd rather keep away from her. We have always been close, even in the two years since she married John, and — suddenly I'm a little afraid of my sister's level grey eyes looking at me, of her questions I don't want to answer.

"Timmy's fine," my mother replies, and her voice, always warm, is even warmer.

"He's got two teeth now, Jane, and he's crawling all over the place." There is laughter in her voice now.

"I wish you could see Dad with him — he was always so sensible and practical with you and Beth when you were babies. But I don't think I've ever seen such a fond grandad."

She opens the kitchen door and puts some water in the kettle, while I take my things up to my old room.

I sit on the bed, and I think about my sister and her baby.

We've talked about children, Rick and I, and we've decided we're not going to have any.

"And then," Rick sometimes says lightly, "when you tire of me and I tire of you, we can thank each other and — move on. No ties, no commitments. No strings attached."

No strings attached, I echo, and I hope that my words don't sound hollow. He is right, of course. We will have our love while it is new and shining, and we won't be forced to hang on when the wonder and the magic have gone.

"And if we don't tire of each other?" I asked him once, carefully.

He shrugged and looked down at me, with laughter in his dark eyes.

"Then we stay together, that's all," he told me.

And then, suddenly serious, suddenly unsmiling, he went on:

"But we'll stay together because we *want* to, Jane, not because we're bound together by a piece of paper and a gold ring."

Suddenly I find myself thinking, inexplicably, of Timmy's christening.

Most of the time he was very good, lying in my arms. But when the water touched his forehead, he gave one surprised little yelp, and looked up at the minister with such reproach on his face that we all smiled.

I remember then that I turned to Beth, but she and John were looking at each other and there was so much loving and closeness there that tears sprang to my eyes.

I stand up briskly, and I remind myself not to be sentimental.

All right, babies are nice, and it's lovely that Mum and Dad are so proud of their grandson, but for Rick and me the choice is made.

We want the freedom to choose our own lifestyle, and it just doesn't include children or marriage, that's all.

COMING, Mum," I reply when my mother calls up that coffee is ready, and I hastily open my suitcase and take out the box of marzipan fruits I've brought with me.

Dad loves them, but usually I only remember to bring them on his birthday. But this morning, on the way to the station, I asked Rick to take me round to the delicatessen to get a box.

"Jane, you remembered," my mother says with pleasure when I put them down on the table.

Remembered? My eyes fly to the calendar, and now I *do* remember. But my face has given me away, and my mother burst out laughing.

"You mean you didn't remember it's our anniversary on Thursday, you just happened to bring them today?"

"I'm sorry, Mum," I say, really upset, for I've always remembered their wedding anniversary, since I was old enough to understand what it meant. I think quickly.

"It's your twenty-fourth, isn't it?" I ask.

"Silver Wedding next year," she agrees, and without asking me, she hands me two of her home-made biscuits.

"Special party?" I ask, teasing her a little, putting off the moment of telling her.

"Are you hiring a room in the hotel?"

"Depends," she replies, stirring her coffee, and I see, with a pang, that there are a few more grey hairs now, as she bends her head.

"Depends on whether we can afford it. Remembering what Beth's wedding cost, if we have another before then we might have to make do with a family party at home!"

This is when I should tell her, I know that. Absurdly, my hands are trembling and I clasp them together to try to steady them. It isn't very successful.

"I wouldn't worry about that," I say. My voice sounds too light and too high.

She looks at me, so sharply that I have to turn away, bending down to pat the dog, who has come to lie at my feet.

"I thought you were seeing quite a lot of this Rick that you mentioned," she says.

"I — do see quite a lot of him," I agree carefully. "But that doesn't mean I'm going to marry him."

No, I think with certainty, it doesn't. It means I love him, it means he loves me, but that doesn't always lead to marriage nowadays.

Suddenly, all the laughter has gone from her eyes, and she puts her hand across the table over mine.

"Jane — he isn't married, is he?" she asks quietly.

I shake my head.

"No," I tell her with complete truth. "He isn't married."

She smiles, but the shadow hasn't left her eyes.

"If he was," she says to me, "if he had led you on and deceived you — I don't know what I'd do to him!"

She looks so small and fierce, like a small brown bird with its feathers ruffled in anger, that I have to smile.

And the moment is gone, the moment when I might have told her.

Continued on page 91

THE GOOD
COMPANIONS

IT must have been well after two o'clock when I awoke out of an uneasy sleep to hear the puppy howling. Rain dashed against the windows, and in the warmth of our comfortable bedroom I shivered when the banshee wail came again.

Poor little thing, to be out on such a night. Lost, I supposed, or abandoned. Leaping out of bed I opened the window to peer out into the teeming darkness. Wind seized the curtains, and whirled them in a wild, ferocious dance — and there was nothing to be seen.

"What is it?" my husband asked sleepily. "Come to bed, mad woman . . ." Suddenly aware of all the centrally-heated air flying out into the wild night, he sat up, wide awake. Once more the pitiful cry sounded, though more faintly this time.

"Listen!" I cried, anguished. "Oh, listen!" and I reached for my dressing-gown.

In spite of his tough, rugby-playing image, my husband is as soft as anything. I could hear, through his complaints, anxiety, as he searched for a vanished slipper.

"Put on your slacks," he ordered me, disappearing downstairs, fastening his dressing-gown as he went. "Wrap up properly . . ."

We found torches and stumbled about in the streaming dark, shining them into the bushes as the wet oozed through my slippers.

Just as we thought we'd have to give up, my husband suddenly shouted, "Here! I've got him!" Pushing the straggling hair out of my eyes, I followed the beam of his torch and I saw him reach into the bushes to hook out the miserable bundle.

Dripping all over the kitchen floor, the little creature crouched close to the stove. We looked at each other and laughed, partly in triumph of rescuing the young dog, and partly at the comical picture we presented.

We sat at the table drinking Christmas sherry — it's not every night we go chasing round a dripping garden — and watched the small grey and white dog gulp mince hungrily, and wash it down with hot milk.

By MARGARET WEST

We couldn't just leave it outside in the rain and the dark. But how would a spoilt, bossy cat react to having a stray puppy in the house?

"Shall we keep him?" I asked coaxingly, for already I had fallen for the fluffy bundle, the little square face, the cool grey-blue eyes.

"Let's call him Sam."

"Someone may be looking for him," my husband pointed out. "Besides how can we? What about Tiger Lily?"

I'd forgotten about our beautiful four-year-old cat, who thought that the house and everything in it was for her exclusive comfort. I looked up from my knees, beside the puppy, over to Tiger's chair. She hadn't moved all this time, and now she regarded us disapprovingly.

THERE were no inquiries for Sam, who grew large and shambling. He had a good deal of the Old English Sheepdog in him and was the gentlest, silliest thing you ever saw in your life. But the pottiest thing of all was the way he let himself be bossed around by the tiny cat!

Then one night Tiger Lily didn't come home. We searched around, called, but to no avail.

Sam was frantic. It took all our coaxing to get him indoors that night.

Next day we took him on his lead. We hoped he would lead us to Tiger Lily, but there was neither sight nor sound of the little cat. Nor had anyone seen her. We were afraid to let Sam off his lead for fear we might lose him, too. He was inconsolable.

NEXT night, as dusk was falling, I went sadly to bring him in for the night. But the garden was empty! Against all likelihood he had jumped the high fence and was gone.

It must have been about five in the morning, three nights after he'd disappeared, when we heard his deep, baying bark at the front door. He wouldn't come in, nor scarcely take time to eat the dish of food we placed before him. He'd found Tiger, we were sure.

Hastily we threw on slacks and sweaters, and fastening Sam's lead, let him take us through the little wood at the back of the house.

Suddenly, just off the track, there she was held fast in a trap. Her leg lay limp and useless and she looked at us from eyes that held only a spark of life. I stroked poor Tiger Lily while my husband freed the mangled limb.

"Don't take on so," he said, and his lips were set and hard. "Perhaps she'll be all right." But we both knew that her chances were slim.

Nor did the vet hold out much hope. "Shock," he said. "And that leg . . ." He shook his head. "That will have to come off."

We took her home, placed her on a cushion by the fire, and watched her sorrowfully. She was pitifully thin and her breath was very light. Sam moved around her anxiously, snuffling softly.

"I'm going to put her in Sam's basket," I decided. "If she's going to die, she might as well be where she most likes."

Sam never left her side and against all predictions Tiger slowly gained strength. Soon she was getting around, bossy as ever, on three legs.

There were no more expeditions to the village; they were content not to venture farther than the garden. But, it soon became plain that she was failing fast.

So we weren't really surprised when, a year after she lost her leg, Sam came in from the garden howling. We found her lifeless under the tree. She must have died in her sleep.

Another year has passed, and once again the air is heavy with summer sweetness. I can see Sam now from the window, lying under the tree. His nose is on his paws and his eyes are dreamy. He doesn't seem to fret any more. I think he knows he won't have very long to wait. ∎

Continued from page 87

"Bring him home with you some time," she says casually. "We'd like to meet him."

"I'll do that," I agree, and I think — that's if you still want him here after I've told you.

"Feel like walking over to Beth's?" my mother asks then. "Or should we take the car?"

"Let's walk," I say. "It's a lovely day."

Walking to Beth's takes quite a time, for the dog wants to come with us, and we have to put him on his lead through the main street.

And, of course, we keep meeting people my mother knows, for we have lived here in this small town all my life.

"Janie — how lovely to see you," Aunt Dora Waters says, hugging me. She isn't really my aunt, of course, but we've always called her that.

"Are you coming round to visit me?"

"I'll try to," I tell her, meaning it, "but I haven't got much time, Aunt Dora, I go back tomorrow."

And then I look at her more closely, and suddenly I see how pale and how old she's become.

"I — I'll be round in the afternoon," I say, not quite steadily.

When we have left her, I turn to my mother and I don't have to say anything.

"Dora Waters is just about the bravest woman I know," she tells me, and her eyes are bright with tears. "Since Tom died five years ago, she's been so lonely."

She looks up at me. "Do make the time to go round, Jane," she says soberly.

"She's got all her family, all her friends," I point out.

HEAVEN SCENT

My life has just taken on a new dimension. Have I won the pools? No, but it's just as exciting.

I have recently come out of hospital after an operation which resulted in me acquiring a sense of smell.

For the first time in my life I have delighted in the scents of flowers, enjoyed the appetising odours of home baking, and appreciated the enjoyment contained within a bottle of perfume.

How dull my "odour-free" life was before!

"Yes, but her husband is gone," my mother replies simply. And then she's her usual brisk self again. "I think we'd better ask Beth to make us some toasted cheese. It must be years since the three of us had lunch together."

We're out of the main street now, and I think of what my mother has just said, and for the first time it dawns on me how changed her life must be now. *Continued on page 95*

GRETNA GREEN
Where Romance Forged Ahead

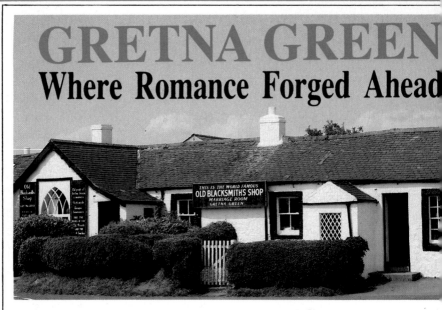

By SONIA ROBERTS

EVEN today, such is the aura of romance which lingers over the otherwise very ordinary border village of Gretna Green, that every year over 60,000 tourists pause in their tours of Scotland to visit the scene of many elopements which found a happy ending here.

Tradition has it that Gretna runaways were wed by a blacksmith using his anvil as an altar. But the myth of the blacksmith "priest" was an English invention.

It stemmed from an operetta of the 1780s which set the scene of an "unofficial" Scottish marriage in a farrier's shop.

By 1843 when Thomas Little of the Queen's Head Inn, Gretna, was improving his premises with an eye to attracting even more runaway weddings, the idea had become so rooted in public imagination that he used a painting of a couple being married "over the anvil" as his sign.

Many of the local inhabitants, despite the prosperity it brought, heartily disapproved of the marriage business and they protested at its lack of authenticity. Mr Little, however, replied that the English were his best customers and an anvil wedding was what they expected to see.

Under old Scottish law, all that a couple had to do to become man and wife was to pledge that intention before witnesses. Such marriages were legal whether performed in the open air or indoors. Indeed, for many of the poorer elopers the ceremony was performed under the arches of Gretna Bridge or out in the hillside above the town.

Most of the would-be brides and 'grooms from England were not poor, however, but well-to-do. They had to be, in an era when transport costs, even over a few miles' distance, were very expensive.

Therefore, those who had made the dash by the fastest post chaise from London to Gretna were hardly likely to quibble about spending

Marriages are made in heaven — and for over a hundred years, heaven for many eloping couples was a small village in the Scottish borders.

he famous old Blacksmith's Anvil. Where Marriages was and still is performed over.

the odd shilling or two extra on arrival. Local hotels soon developed a daunting range of "extras" for the trimmings of runaway marriages.

In August 1825 when John Bell and Mary Hakinson, both of Bolton, were married at the Gretna Hall Hotel, they were later presented with a bill for:

Wine and brandy, 3s 2d.
Breakfast, 4s 6d.
Post Boy's Meal, 5s.
Horse's Hay, 2s.
Witnesses, £2 2s.
Wedding Room, 10s 6d.

As well as these obvious charges, the bridegroom might well have to budget for generous tips to servants and stable staff all along the runaway route. Such bribes would ensure that the bridal party did indeed get the fastest horses available and possibly that their pursuers were put off the scent.

THIS was an age when, on marriage, a bride handed over all her worldly wealth to her husband, with no financial or legal safeguards for her own future, so rich fathers were understandably more chary than they are today of their daughters falling into the hands of unscrupulous fortune hunters.

Often they were prepared to take the most desperate steps to halt the elopers.

When in May 1782, Sarah Child, daughter of a London banker, eloped with the son of the Earl of Westmorland, the angry father shot the leading horse of the bridal carriage to bring it to a halt.

The quick thinking of the bridegroom's servant saved the day. He not only managed to cut the dead animal free of the reins, thus allowing the lovers to get away in a three instead of a four-horse carriage. At the same time he slashed the straps which fastened the body of the father's carriage to its springs.

So when the disgruntled Mr Child tried to resume his journey, his carriage collapsed beneath him. By the time he managed to hire a replacement, the couple had got to Gretna and married.

You might think that after such an eventful start to their own married life the Earl and Countess might have looked kindly on other elopers in the future.

Not so, for when their own daughter wanted to marry the Earl of Jersey, she, too, had to bolt for the border followed by a very outraged father.

It was not always fathers who had the unenviable task of making a breakneck dash to prevent a marriage they disapproved of.

Sometimes, mothers were cast in this rôle. And you cannot, for example, help but have some sympathy for the case of Sophia Stanley's mother.

Sophie was just 13 when in May 1815 she absconded from her smart boarding school with a Captain

Bontein of the Guards. He was a twice-married widower, aged 44, with no income beyond a half-pay pension.

However, Sophia was by no means the youngest of Gretna brides of this era.

In 1854, another schoolgirl, Anne Jane Ward, aged just 12, ran away to Gretna with the music teacher of her school. The couple were caught on their way back from Gretna at Carlisle railway station.

The husband, John Atkinson, was tried for abducting a minor and jailed for nine months. His child bride, meanwhile, was sent to Jersey to "forget the whole unfortunate incident," while all over Britain, High Court judges were squabbling as to whether the marriage was indeed valid.

Anne Jane, however, refused to forget her husband. As soon as he was free she made her way north and re-married him in the parish church at Appleby.

They lived happily together until his death in 1870 and had seven children.

John Atkinson was lucky his sentence was so light. Edward Gibbon Wakefield, who married 16-year-old schoolgirl Ellen Turner at Gretna in 1826, received a three-year jail sentence.

But whereas John and Anne Jane seem to have been genuinely in love, court proceedings clearly revealed that Edward Wakefield had more a financial than romantic interest in his wife.

Sometimes in their attempts to avoid pursuit, Gretna-bound lovers would don bizarre disguises.

When, in October 1818, Lord Erskine decided to make an honest woman of his mistress, Sarah, by whom he already had several children, he dressed in women's clothes to avoid being spotted during the long journey north to Gretna.

It was only at the insistence of the offical performing the ceremony that Lord Erskine was persuaded to remove his petticoats while making his vows. The children who had accompanied their parents north discreetly hid themselves under their mother's cloak.

There was a new twist to the usual story, however. It was Lord Erskine's teenage son, by his first marriage, who dashed to Gretna to try to prevent the love affair being legalised. But he arrived in the village just a fraction too late.

Yet another eager husband-to-be arrived disguised as a chimney sweep, and was only persuaded to clean up for the ceremony when his wife tearfully complained she couldn't recognise him beneath the dirt!

The heyday of Gretna was from 1754 to 1856. English law on marriage was tightened up in 1754 and so caused a flood of runaways to Scotland where rules remained laxer. Then in 1856 legislation came into force which brought Scottish law closer to English, demanding a longer residential qualification. And so the number of Gretna weddings per year were reduced considerably.

In 1855, the last year in which old law applied, 707 Gretna marriages were recorded. By 1907, the famous "smithy" had become a museum and gifts shop.

It all ended during the Second World War. The last couple to be married in the old Scottish style were James Tod of Stirling and Annie Colquhoun. And they just made it. They arrived at the Gretna smithy one hour before the 350-year-old marriage law became invalid! ■

Continued from page 91

"Isn't it strange, just you and Dad at home?" I ask her curiously.

She turns to look at me, and there is something in her brown eyes that makes me suddenly uncomfortable, knowing what I am going to tell her.

"It was at first," she says thoughtfully. "But you must remember, Jane, we had time to become used to the idea.

"First Beth went away nursing, but you were still at home. Then when you were at college Beth was working at the hospital here, and by the time you moved into the flat in town, Beth and John were married and living here. It all happened so gradually that we had time to get used to it."

She smiled. "And you know, you may find this hard to believe at your age, but there is something very pleasant and peaceful about this time of life. I'm forty-five, Jane, your father is forty-seven. That probably seems old to you, but — to me, your father still seems the same young man I married twenty-four years ago. The same, only — so much dearer, because of the years together."

For a moment, my breath catches in my throat and I wonder if she knows, and is trying to say something to me. But the thought passes.

How could she know?

Yet, I am strangely touched, for my mother has never before spoken to me like this. The disturbing thought comes to me, though. Will Rick and I grow older together? Will we stay with each other long enough for me one day to feel as my mother feels? And then I remind myself fiercely of the things we've said. We will stay together only if we want to, not because we *have* to.

The dog, suddenly realising where we are, bounds ahead of us and with a sudden resurgence of youth, he jumps over the low wall outside Beth's house.

Timmy's pram is under the apple tree, and I follow my mother over to it. He is asleep, one chubby starfish hand pushed into his cheek. I'm surprised how much more hair he has since I saw him a few weeks ago. And I am surprised, too, at the wave of love for my small nephew that sweeps over me.

Beth hurries out, and we hug each other quickly. Both of us are a little ashamed of the depth of family and sisterly feeling that always comes over us. She is wearing jeans and one of John's shirts, and it is only when she turns to take us inside, that I wonder.

"Beth?" I ask her as we go into the big sunny kitchen.

I don't need to say any more, and colour floods her face.

"Thanks for not telling her, Mum," she says, and her face lights up.

"Isn't it lovely, Jane? We'd quite like another boy this time, since they'll be so close."

"So close!" I say, teasing her a little. "But Timmy isn't even a year old yet."

"He's ten months," Beth replies equably, "and we want to have our four all together." *Continued on page 97*

" And " I Quote ...

VICTORIA WOOD (1953) was born in Lancashire, and holds a university degree in Drama. She has often appeared on TV and on stage both solo and in her own humorous sketches; also occasionally with her husband, a magician (The Great Soprendo).

I toured the working-men's clubs with a magic act; I used to close with a song. When I got better at it I used to saw myself in half and finish with a duet.

I think we were more neighbourly in those days. If anyone was ill in bed, the whole street would let themselves in and ransack the parlour.

"Has he got over his divorce?"
"I think so. His wife got custody of the stereo and they sold the children."

" And " I Quote ...

CYRIL FLETCHER (1913), English variety comedian, pantomime actor, radio and TV performer, regularly appeared in "That's Life." His own writing features the "Odd Ode."

For many years I was quite sure that thunder was the sound of God moving his beer barrels across the floor of the sky.

Our first domestic servant seemed to be an old English sheepdog in maid's uniform, who needed to keep her feet up as much as possible.

I have a large voice. Large enough to fill the Albert Hall; or empty it.

Continued from page 95

She pushes a kitchen stool to me, and I sit down.

"Don't marry an only child, Jane," she warns, smiling. "John just has this idea that Timmy is going to be part of a big family!"

Rick is an only child, too, I think, but he doesn't feel the way John does, concerning families.

We talk of this small town we all love, and of the friends we have known all our lives. Then my mother hears Timmy in his pram, and she goes out to bring him in.

He is rosy and sleepy, and all at once a little shy when he sees me. But I talk to him, and I think he remembers my voice, and soon holds out his arms and comes to me.

I have forgotten the feel and smell of a warm sleepy baby in my arms, the softness of his hair against my cheek and the surprising strength of his sturdy little legs as he stands up on my knee.

Suddenly, bewilderingly, I know that I can't bear to have him in my arms any longer, and I put him down on the kitchen floor.

I love my sister, and my small nephew, but now all I want is to get out of here. Away from this comfortable, slightly untidy kitchen with John's old jacket hanging on the back door, with Timmy's jars of

---

ON THE RIGHT TRACK

We arrived at the station just in time to see our train pullng away. My husband was obviously annoyed with me and said:

"If you hadn't taken so long getting yourself ready, we would have caught that train."

I felt rather guilty and was about to say how sorry I was, when my young daughter saved the day!

"Yes, Daddy," she interrupted, "but if you hadn't hurried us along, we wouldn't have had to wait so long for the next one!"

---

baby food lined up in the cupboard. With its whole atmosphere of marriage.

My mother and Beth are surprised when I say I think we should go, but I remind my mother that I promised to visit Aunt Dora.

"Goodbye, Jane," Beth says as we leave her. "Bring Rick down sometime soon — does he play golf? John is always looking for someone to have a game with."

I realise, with a little surprise, that I really don't know whether Rick plays golf or not.

WE don't talk much on the way home. I find all at once that it's difficult to talk about anything, and I'm finding it harder and harder to say the thing I came here to say.

But my mother — I don't know, I realise, as I look at her walking along beside me. I don't know why she is silent, too.

The afternoon passes, with a short visit to Aunt Dora, and we come back home, both of us still quiet. My mother asks if I want to go out for a meal, but I tell her I'd rather just stay at home.

And I think, knowing I am being a coward, that it would be better to say nothing now. Better to let her go ahead with the meal she is making, better, too, to meet my father and — to have, at least, a little while with him unspoiled by what I am going to say to them.

He is a quiet man, my father, but we have always been close, he and I.

When he comes home we walk around the garden together while my mother is busy in the kitchen. We don't talk much, but then we never do. I have never felt that the silence between us is awkward, and yet now I find myself talking more than usual, telling him about my work, about Beth, about Timmy.

Sometimes I find his eyes — grey and level — resting on me, with a question in them. And it is a question that I find I don't want to answer.

He shows me the roses, and we stand together under the oak tree, looking at the swing.

"Have to get new ropes before young Timmy starts using it," my father remarks, touching the swing, unused for so long. He smiled at me.

"Do you remember when you pushed Beth out of the swing, Jane?"

I remember, and I remember, too, the terror when Beth lay on the ground, unmoving. I climbed down from the tree and I rushed to her.

She opened her eyes, I remember, and said clearly, "If I die, you're not to have the dolls' house, or my dolls."

We talk of this, my father and I, smiling as we remember, and my father tells me that he still has the dolls' house out in the garage, ready to work on if Beth's new baby should be a girl.

THE DARK AGES?

As I look around at the modern offices of today, I can't help comparing them with the office I worked in during the Thirties.

We had to have electric lights on all day, as windows were too small to let in much daylight. I used to dread having to look up old files, as they were kept in a basement where rats used to scamper around.

Our "rest room" boasted a broken settee and a rickety card table.

Now when I see bright, airy offices, with exotic plants on window-sills, I often wish I was starting my career all over again.

"My father made it for you girls, of course," he reminds me.

He shakes his head. "Funny, fathers don't really have time to do that sort of thing for their own children, they have to wait for their grandchildren."

He is not a demonstrative man, and I am a little surprised when he puts his arm around my shoulders and hugs me, briefly.

"When your children come along, Jane, I'll have time to make things for them, too."

Unexpectedly, my eyes blur with tears, and I turn away, saying that I must go and help Mum. And while I set the table for the three of us, I remind myself fiercely how wonderful it's going to be, Rick and me on our own. No more hurrying away from each other, no more leaving each other when we want to stay together.

"When did you get this old picture out?" I ask my mother, when I open the sideboard to get out the salt and pepper. There I am, at 17, my face plumper than it is now, my hair tied back and my eyes wide and serious.

My mother comes through from the kitchen and takes it from me, studying it.

"I don't think I'll ever forget that," she murmurs, half to herself.

"That night, when we came to the prizegiving, we knew you were to be made a prefect, but we didn't know until the last minute that you were Head Girl. I was so proud, Jane — no matter what happens, I'll never forget how proud I was then."

I look down at my mother, and I am certain that she does know. How, I don't understand, but — she is like that, my mother.

"Mum, I —" I begin uncertainly, but I cannot go on. For a moment, we stand looking at each other, and then my father comes in, asking if supper is ready.

STRANGELY enough, in spite of the strain I feel, it is a happy meal. We talk about things that happened years ago, when Beth and I were small, and sometimes my mother and father remember something that happened too far back for me to remember.

"Do you remember the way Beth was when Jane was born, Bill?" my mother asks my father. She turns to me.

"She was quite polite for the first week, and then she came to me one day and said she thought we should take you back, you cried too much, and maybe they'd give us a puppy instead."

We talk then about Timmy, about how he will be with a new baby, and my father thinks they will have less trouble, for Timmy will be only 15 or 16 months when the new baby comes.

"That's what there was between Beth and William," my mother says quietly. They look at each other, and the laughter has gone, and I know that they have forgotten me.

And I am ashamed that I never give a thought to the son they lost, the little boy who lived for only a month. And for the first time I begin to realise that in all these years they have never forgotten this loss.

For a moment, my father's big brown hand covers my mother's, a little awkwardly. And soon she smiles, and they remember that I am there, and we talk of something else. But even late at night, when we are ready to go to bed, my mother's eyes are still bright.

I go round with my father as he closes the doors, after Shep has had his last wander around the garden.

"Do you remember the old swing seat that used to sit on the porch?" my father asks me. He looks around cautiously, but my mother is in the kitchen.

"I've ordered a new one, for our anniversary."

He smiles, and all at once I can see what my mother means when she says that for her he has never changed, because there is a sudden youthfulness about his face.

"We've got more time together now, your mother and I, and we can enjoy sitting on the porch in the swing seat, watching our grandchildren."

When he says that, I feel a stab that is almost a physical pain.

I SAY good night to my parents, and I go up to bed in my old room. I don't expect to sleep well, because there are so many things turning around in my mind. But there is something about the air here, and I find myself becoming drowsy, and then I am in a deep, dreamless sleep.

It's very early when I wake, and everything is still. All at once I cannot stay in bed any longer. I pull on jeans and a shirt, and push my feet into shoes.

Quietly, I tiptoe downstairs and into the kitchen, where Shep's basket is. He is delighted to see someone awake so early. I have to tell him to be quiet as he rushes around the kitchen.

I open the kitchen door, and the dog and I go out into the garden. The grass is wet with dew, and the dog's big paws leave marks on it. No other dog can ever mean as much to me as this one does. I was eight when we got him, he is part of my childhood, part of my growing up. Beth told me yesterday they are getting a puppy soon, for they want their children to grow up with a family dog.

There is the swing that my father is going to mend for Timmy to use, and in the garage is the workbench with the dolls' house sitting on it, waiting. The new swing seat will sit right here, where the old cane chair sits, and my mother and my father will sit on it together, watching Beth's children.

Beth's children. But — not mine, not mine and Rick's, because we don't want that. We will be free, free and unchained by any band of gold, any piece of paper.

I sit down on the old cane chair, and I know, with complete certainty, that I don't want this.

I know now that I want to have Rick's children, I want us to share our laughter and our grief. I want us to have a dog for our children, I want us to grow old together.

I want us to be married.

It's as simple as that.

I don't know what has done it — seeing Timmy, talking to my mother, hearing my father talk of the things he would do for his grandchildren, seeing the way my mother and my father still look at each other, after all these years. Perhaps just coming home.

I don't know, and it doesn't really matter.

All that matters is that today I will tell Rick that I have changed my mind, that I won't be moving in with him. I'll tell him he was right, I am old fashioned. I know that for me the old-fashioned way is right, that it's marriage or nothing.

And as I sit on the porch I shiver a little, although the sun has come up, for I know very well that I might lose Rick. I will try to make him see what I have come to see — that marriage isn't a prison. Love, real love, can be more free when it's encircled by that band of gold.

But perhaps he won't understand, and perhaps that will be the end of Rick and me. If it is, I don't know how I will be able to bear it, I love him so much. But I have to take that chance, for the other way is not right for me.

The door opens and my mother comes out and gives me a cup of tea. She sits down on the other old chair, beside me, and we drink our tea in silence.

Then my mother puts her cup down and looks at me.

"I came down because I thought you wanted to talk to me, Jane," she says directly, and her brown eyes hold mine steadily.

I know, looking at her, that she has prepared herself to take whatever I am going to say without flinching, and my heart aches for the grief and the worry I have given her recently.

Carefully, I put down my cup, too.

"It's all right, Mum," I tell her gently, my voice a little unsteady. "I — I thought I was going to do something, but I've changed my mind."

I will never know if she did realise what I came to tell her, or if I only thought she knew. But now, as I look at her, her eyes clear and she smiles, just a little.

"As long as you know what you're doing," she says to me.

I nod my head.

"Yes," I tell her steadily. "I know what I'm doing."

And I do. Even if it means losing Rick, I know what I'm doing.

"It will work out, Janie," my mother says softly.

I hope so, I think, as I follow her into the kitchen.

I know that nothing will make me change my mind now, for I am completely certain about this. And — perhaps Rick will understand, perhaps he will feel that marriage needn't be what he thought. Perhaps . . .

———————— * **THE END** * ————————

CONFESSION IS GOOD FOR THE SOUL

Their marriage was one year old today. And so, too, was the guilty secret he could keep to himself no longer . . .

WEDDING anniversary or not, I was going to tell Kelly the truth tonight, I decided. I would start the second year of our married life with the slate clean.

She had mentioned our first date once or twice over the past year, each time with a happy little smile on her face. But the fact was, I hadn't played fair, and tonight I felt I must confess.

Kelly would understand — probably even think of what I'd done as a compliment. On the other hand, there was the chance she'd get mad, throw something at me, even!

Anyway, I had to tell her, and get the facts straight. It had been on my conscience too long.

We'd decided to have our first anniversary dinner at home, with the lace-edged linen cloth Kelly's gran had embroidered for us and our best, special-occasion cutlery and wine goblets.

"Next time we have all this lot out will be the christening," Kelly said that evening, patting her tummy, and added with a grimace, "Don't suppose we'll manage all this gracious living next year. Especially if it's twins, as the doctor suspects!"

"Just picture us," I said and smiled, "each with a howling baby on our knee, drinking a toast in gripe water!"

Kelly frowned.

"You're happy about it, though, Hugh?"

"Of course I am, darling."

Kelly picked up her glass of wine. "Talking of toasts — we haven't had one," she said. "What'll we drink to? The twins?"

"Yes, but first, Kelly, here's to you, love."

Kelly smiled radiantly. "And here's to you, darling."

She clinked her glass against mine and laughed happily.

We finished our meal and the last of the wine, and carried the dishes to the kitchen.

"I'll wash up in a minute," I said hastily and steered her in to the lounge.

I took a deep breath. "There's something I've got to tell you, Kelly. It's a . . . well . . . a kind of confession I've got to make, about something I did soon after we first met. A — a sort of deception." I cleared my throat.

Kelly looked at me, alarmed.

"Well, in that case, I'm going to make the coffee first," she said and disappeared into the kitchen.

I sat there, rehearsing my opening words. "Kelly, darling, remember that first time we met?"

How could I ever forget it . . . ?

102

**Complete
Story By
STELLA
BLAINEY**

IT was summertime, and I was
planting lettuce seeds in old Mr
Hudson's garden. Bob
Hudson's our next-door neighbour.
We were both living alone in those
days, and had a very amicable
comradeship over the garden fence
— in spite of the difference in our
ages.

Bob's wife had died while I was
still a small boy and I couldn't
remember her very clearly. His two
married daughters came to stay
occasionally.

One lived in Canada and the other
had married a Devonshire farmer.

Once a year, Bob went down to
Devon for a month and he had left
for there only the morning before
the particular day I was thinking of.

I'd carried his case for him to the
station, a 10-minute walk away, and
throughout that walk, Bob worried
about his garden.

"All this packin' and messin' about
— I never even got any lettuce
planted," he grumbled. "Now you
will clip the hedge for me, won't
you, Hugh?"

"Don't worry about a thing, Bob."
I nodded and shifted the suitcase to
my other hand.

"Just the hedge now. Leave everything else."

I couldn't blame him for that
remark. The year before, I'd been
moved to do a bit of weeding for
him — pulling up some of his highly-
prized plants in the process.

I was no gardener in those days.
When I'd lost both my parents a few
years earlier, I had kept the house
but had slowly let the garden go
wild, lacking the heart to bother with
it, staving off my loneliness with
hour after hour of study.

"You shouldn't have neglected her like that," Bob had chided me. "Broke yer dad's heart it would've done to see her like that."

He'd puffed his pipe fiercely, sending clouds of smoke over the fence.

"I haven't time for it," I'd answered airily. "What with all this housework, cooking, *and* my studying."

I didn't tell him my "domestic work" consisted of an occasional brief whirl round with the vacuum cleaner and a swipe at the furniture with a duster once a week, and my "cooking" was mostly confined to opening tins and visiting the fish and chip shop.

I think he knew, though, for on Sundays he had me round to dinner and we always had steak, a small roast, or his speciality, oxtail stew.

"When you get through those dispensin' exams, you'll have to do somethin' about her," he'd growl, casting his eyes over my untidy tangle of long grass and weeds.

When I did pass my exams and got a job at a branch chemist's in our small Northern town, I made some effort at weeding and mowing now and then, to please old Bob.

THE day after I'd seen Bob off at the station, I had to make a journey myself, to Ransley, a biggish city some 50 miles away, where the chemist's I worked for had a large, busy branch.

Holidays and sickness among the staff there had created a temporary crisis and I was on loan to them for a month.

I'd decided to stay in the city during the week and had found temporary digs. I would travel back on Saturday after work to spend Sundays at home and keep an eye on my place and Bob's.

On the first Saturday, just before we closed, I had a sudden inspiration, and bought a packet of lettuce seeds from the gardening department.

I'd plant them in Bob's vegetable patch, I thought, visualising his delight when he returned to a row of beautiful green lettuces, flourishing beside his beetroots and onions.

A couple of hours later, I was making holes with a piece of cane, dropping in seeds with careless abandon and whistling, when a voice said:

"You're planting those far too deeply. Too close together as well. Can't you read the instructions?"

Startled, I looked up into a pair of the darkest blue eyes I'd ever seen. Their owner was leaning over Bob's end fence, where a public footpath ran between the fields and the backs of our gardens.

I gazed at this slip of a girl who was frowning at my back-to-the-land efforts, trying to place her in my mind. For I knew I'd seen her before.

"Where've I . . . ?" I began.

"On the seven o'clock train from Ransley." She read my thoughts.

"Ah, yes." I nodded. "You were farther up the carriage, reading a book. You seemed very absorbed."

"It was a gardening book. I help Dad on Sundays. Mum doesn't like gardening at all."

"That makes two of us." I stood up, rubbing my cramped legs. "But even *I* can plant a few lettuce seeds for a neighbour. There's nothing to it."

"Oh, but there is," she protested. "They need to be a certain depth, and . . ." She glanced at the packet on the ground beside me.

"Those pelleted seeds have to be planted the right distance apart. They don't need thinning, but they do need watering well if it doesn't rain. Otherwise they won't come up at all."

"Nonsense." I was stung by the cool superiority of her tone. "This time next week there'll be a nice row of lettuces here, thrusting their little green heads to the sky."

"Really?" Her perfectly-shaped brown eyebrows shot up. "Want to bet?" She seemed highly amused.

"Yes," I said firmly. "I'll bet you a box of chocolates to a . . ."
I thought for a moment, then had a brilliant idea:
" . . . to a date for an evening out."

"Done!" She grinned. "I'll see you here this time next week. By the way, I prefer plain chocolates to milk."

I came over to the fence.

"I'll probably see you on the seven o'clock on Saturday. I take it you work in Ransley?"

"Yes, I'm at Allam's," she said, naming a big department store. "Book section. See you, then."

She waved a hand and went on her way.

Monday, Tuesday and Wednesday of the next week I sweltered in Ransley, as the sun shone fiercely from a sky of paint-box blue and my prayers for rain went unanswered. If Miss Know-It-All was right about the need for plenty of water, my seeds would be getting nowhere fast.

THEN I got a break, and so did the weather. All day Thursday we had thunderstorms and torrential rain, enough for the thirstiest seed-pellet, and I visualised my little protégées popping tender heads through the soil to the great big world above.

I took the precaution of telephoning Mrs Manning, Bob's neighbour on the other side, however, during my lunch break on Friday. I asked her if she'd noticed whether old Bob's lettuces were up yet.

I gave her no reason for my sudden concern and she must have thought it strange, but she obligingly went to look, getting back to the phone just in time to tell me there was "not a sign of them" before the pips went.

I went back towards the shop thoughtfully, making a diversion down a small side street to a gardening shop, and there my luck was in. For among the trays of seedlings I found a box of tiny plants marked "Lettuce" and, with only a small twinge of conscience, bought them.

I knew I'd have to make the journey home that evening, for I'd never be able to conceal them from a certain pair of blue eyes on the train the following day.

I made it to the station without a moment to spare, climbing aboard the train seconds before it left, and sank thankfully into a seat in the last compartment, clutching my box of plants tightly to me.

Once home, I stayed indoors till the light was fading, then I nipped round to Bob's, got a trowel from his shed and did some not-very-expert planting. I felt furtively pleased with myself as I gave the seedlings a good watering before catching the last train back to Ransley.

I reached the station in good time next evening, spotting my betting partner as she arrived carrying her weekend case, and we sat together chatting throughout the journey, swapping names and potted life histories.

Neither of us referred to our wager until we got off the train, when she said goodbye, adding:

"I'll be round for my chocolates later."

By the time she knocked I had showered and changed into my favourite shirt and new jeans and had a pot of coffee percolating nicely on the kitchen stove.

I opened the door wide and ushered her in, my heart pounding suddenly at the sight of her in a silky white sweater and blue skirt.

She paused with one foot inside the door.

"Shouldn't we look at Mr . . . er . . . What's-his-name's garden before the sun goes down?"

"Easily done from this side of the fence," I said, ushering her through the kitchen to the back garden.

The sight of my neglected patch must have caused her an inward shudder, but she ignored it and crossed to the right-hand fence through a mass of chickweed and dandelions.

I followed her, peering over her shoulder at my little row of lettuces, carelessly out of alignment, like a platoon of newly-recruited soldiers, but standing nicely to attention in the soil.

"Well, Kelly Anderson, how about that?" I asked, trying not to sound too triumphant.

She whistled. "How *about* that! It's a miracle," she declared.

"They happen sometimes."

I made a mental note to ask Mrs Manning to water them for me if the weather was dry, and to get a cloche from Bob's shed and cover them. I had no intention of letting the birds benefit from all my efforts!

We went back into the house and had coffee and I arranged to take her to the Gun and Garter for a meal next day. I walked her home and she offered to come round early next morning and help me make a start on my own disgrace of a garden.

"For with fingers that are positively emerald," she murmured sweetly, "it would be sinful to neglect your talent."

Crafty little monkey!

THE garden looks nice now, I must admit, and though I started straightening it up to please Kelly, I take quite a pride in it these days.

Just then Kelly brought in the coffee, and between sips, I told her the story of my shameful behaviour in the affair of the lettuce plants. Or rather, I told it to her back.

She had turned to look out of the window at the roses, nodding their velvet heads around a fresh-cut lawn in the evening sun.

She remained that way, still and silent, until I was finished.

Then she turned on me.

"Oh, Hugh, you idiot!" she yelled. "You and your stupid confession. I tried to stop you. Now *I'll* have to own up, too!"

"Own up? You? What to?" I asked, bewildered.

She sat down beside me.

CAUGHT IN THE ACT

One day, after posting a letter at the post office, I peeped down the chute to make sure it had dropped in safely.

To my surprise and shock, I saw a pair of eyes looking right back at me out of the darkness. Then, the owner of the eyes gave a naughty little wink and vanished back behind his hatch!

I often wonder whether he was as surprised as I was, or maybe it was his way of getting a new outlook on things!

"I never would have told you, but I knew all about those lettuce plants."

"You *knew*? Oh — you guessed, I suppose. Was that it?"

Kelly still does all our planting, while I content myself with

Continued on page 114

Never An Idle Moment!

Forget the notion that girls of yesteryear were fragile creatures — they had a tough timetable to govern their lives!

By Roy Brink-Budgen

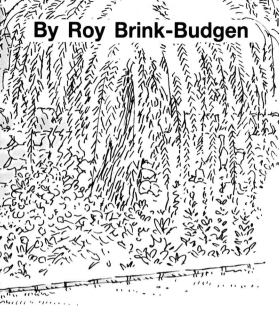

SEVENTY-FIVE years ago, a girl did not have to worry about wet afternoons or long school holidays. Not for her the passive pleasures of the television or personal stereo. For, having persuaded her mother to buy a copy of "Three Hundred And One Things A Bright Girl Can Do," her days would then be more than filled.

Anything from knitting a tennis net, to making a calendar out of a tambourine, making Siberian coffee or decorating a cathedral. In all, 301 things to keep her happy and busy.

So, by using her book, how might a bright girl in 1914 fill her day? As she wakes in the morning, what has she got planned? Before breakfast, of course, she must check that her bedroom is neat.

Her bedroom done, she checks the date on her calendar made out of a tambourine covered with embroidered linen and, walking gracefully with a small bag of dried peas on her head, descends the stairs for breakfast.

Having kept some of the hard-boiled eggs for decoration later, she finishes her breakfast (keeping her bag of peas upon her head), and goes to feed her silkworms with some white mulberry leaves.

IT is a sunny morning, so our girl goes into the garden. Though much of the work in a garden is "not appropriate for a lady," there is still plenty for her to do.

She has some seeds to plant which she obtained, of course, only from a seedsman with a good character. Some she plants in her own herbaceous border, whilst others she plants in a window box which she made out of a packing case, drainage holes being made with a red-hot poker.

This done, as the book recommends, she looks around for a clean barrel. Having found one, she skilfully dismantles it, drills some holes with a brace and bit and, using 20 feet of stout rope, she transforms this barrel into a hammock.

She ties the completed hammock between two trees, puts a few cushions upon it, and watches as her brother, being much less energetic and resourceful, climbs on to it to read a magazine.

Dismantling a barrel is thirsty work for our bright girl. So, as a just reward, she goes to the kitchen for a drink. Not for her the coloured fizz from the supermarket shelf, but a wide choice of home-made delights.

namon to taste and on[e]
teaspoonful of ginge[r]
essence. She then straine[d]
it and bottled it. Super.

There is still plenty o[f]
time before lunch to deco[r]
ate those hard-boiled egg[s]
and also to make a puppe[t]
for her puppet theatre. Sh[e]
boils some logwood for [a]
purple egg, boils anothe[r]
with onions to colour [it]
amber, and a third wit[h]
spinach juice to make [it]
green.

She wants to write a[n]
inscription on a fourth o[ne]
so she fashions a piece o[f]
mutton suet into a pen[c]
and writes her messag[e]
upon the warm egg. Ha[v]
ing dipped it into cochinea[l]
the inscription remain[s]
whilst the rest of the eg[g]
turns red. Leaving them o[ut]
to dry, she turns her atte[n]
tion to her puppet.

Will it be Barley Sherbert or Egg Lemonade? Perhaps Cream Nectar or Peppermint Cordial? All very tempting, but she has already decided. It is a refreshing glass of Cinnamonade.

The day before, she boiled one quart of water, and gradually stirred in one ounce of coarsely-ground wheat and the juice of two lemons. (Sometimes she used oranges.) When it was cool, she added cin-

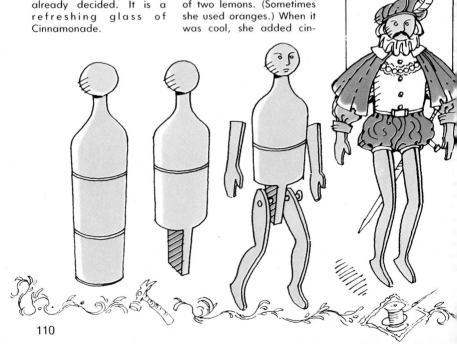

110

She takes a wooden kittle, some wood from a igar box, some pieces of elvet and bits from her agbag. Then, using her imble fingers, she transorms the skittle into a avalier. Simple!

TIME now for lunch. She must not take too long ver this meal, of course, ecause she has a busy fternoon ahead of her. A ew friends have been vited round for games. ut, being a girl who likes ɔ pack as much as posible into her day, she was ot content to write out ach invitation — much too me-consuming.

There fore, she made erself a gelatine pad for eproducing copies, using elatine, glycerine, carbolic cid and water. When the ixture had been prepared nd cooled, she only eeded to write out her ivitation once, and then lace the paper upon the elatine pad. Having transerred the words from aper to pad, she could ɑpidly run off as many ɔpies as she wanted.

Lunch over, she has a little while before her friends arrive. And, as the book suggests, "Girls often wish to cut a bottle in half." She cuts a few bottles by burning paraffin-soaked string around them, then writes a message upon each of the halves using some fluorspar and sulphuric acid which she keeps in her room.

Her friends arrive. There are lots of games to play. They race clothes pegs, play Quakers' meeting, fish pond, engage in thought-reading and instantaneous photography.

Refreshments are served after a game of fans and feathers. Siberian toffee for everyone — and it's so easy to make that our girl made this batch before bedtime the day before. Could this be the fore-runner of "Blue Peter"?

She melted two ounces of butter, two table-spoonfuls of syrup, and two teacupfuls of granulated sugar. She boiled the mixture for a few minutes, then poured in a tin of condensed milk.

Then she boiled the mixture for 20 minutes, stirring all the time. Before pouring the mixture into a buttered tin, she added two tea-spoonfuls of essence of lemon.

The afternoon has been most pleasurable. As her friends leave, she hands each of them a half bottle upon which she had earlier

engraved "Thank you for coming," and each of which contains a few pieces of transparent toffee. (Five pounds of the best brown sugar mixed with four small teacupfuls of water. When the sugar boils, add two teaspoonfuls of the best pale vinegar.)

NOW Mother asks her to put away her toys, so our girl clears everything away, and goes to have afternoon tea. The sandwiches are placed upon a doyley with a thistle border which she crocheted on Monday morning. The tray is covered with a daisy-work cloth which she sewed on Monday afternoon.

Tea over, the day is almost done. She feeds her silkworms, puts her knitted slippers upon her feet, the bag of dried peas upon her head, and walks gracefully to her bedroom.

She quickly makes a photographic mount decorated with bramble leaves, does a couple of sketches to practise the laws of perspective and, having washed and undressed, gets into bed.

As she lies under her trellis-pattern patchwork quilt which she made on Tuesday, she wonders what to do tomorrow. Should she decorate her local cathedral with banners, shields, arcades and stars, or make a sandwich bag out of a one lb. mustard tin?

Perhaps a series of coloured fires in the drawing-room or make a tent out of rotproof, green canvas at only 10d a yard? Perhaps she could learn to swim or row? Make a belt out of melon seeds? No, perhaps it would be more fun to bind a few magazines, make a lampshade, wash a golf jersey, preserve some seaweed. Then, after lunch, what?

But our bright girl is too tired to think more. She falls asleep and dreams of making a macaroni necklace painted with Egyptian hieroglyphics. ∎

Dial "L" For Laughter

JUST picture the scene — a family gather round the telephone in the living-room. There is an air of excitement, mostly generated by Mum. But that's not surprising. After all, the whole thing is her idea.

As the clock approaches "zero hour," Dad is hauled from his favourite chair and the teenage children are told to switch off the stereo.

"I've got the number," Mum says.

A hundred miles away Mum's younger brother, Tom, should just have arrived home to his flat from college.

It's an important day for him. He's away from home and it's his 21st birthday.

The hands of the clock move to "zero hour." Mum picks up the receiver and dials.

She can hear the phone ringing at the other end.

"Ready, everyone," she says, her eyes bright with excitement.

The phone is lifted at the other end. Mum's hand descends. Everyone begins to sing at the top of their voices, "Happy Birthday To You."

Before the last note has died away they go on to "For He's A Jolly Good Fellow," and finish.

Eagerly they await a reaction. There is a long silence on the line. Then a very cultured voice says, "Thank you very much, but I'm afraid you have the wrong number."

And they did, too!

Mum, who is a very dear friend of mine, told me that story the day after it happened.

We laughed over it till the tears ran down our cheeks.

It didn't surprise me, though. Things like that happen to my friend all the time.

They happen to her because she refuses to let life become routine and ordinary. The result is, extraordinary things happen to her.

And I for one envy her.

H

Continued from page 107

digging, mowing and trimming the hedges, so my knowledge of the ways of seeds, pelleted or otherwise, is hazy.

"I would have guessed —" she nodded "— but I knew *before* that. I was on that Friday evening train, too, Hugh."

"*You* were on it?" I must have looked incredulous.

"I was at the front of the train, looking out of the window, when I saw you come charging up at the last moment, clutching your box of seedlings.

"I didn't need Sherlock Holmes to tell me what you were up to, so I stayed on the train till you got off and went out of the station. Then I got the next train back to town."

I realised that I was gawping like a half-wit and closed my mouth. Then I drew her down on to the settee beside me and pulled her close.

"So it was important to you, too, that first date?"

"Well, of course it was, Hugh! I never would have told you I'd seen you," she repeated.

"Wait a minute . . ."

As I began to get over the surprise she'd sprung on me, two questions sprang to the front of my mind. I had to know the answers to both.

"In the first place." I asked, "what were *you* doing on that Friday evening train?"

She blushed. "If you must know," she said, "I had a box of lettuce plants, too."

"You did? Oh, Kelly, darling. And why did those lettuce seeds I planted never come up?"

Kelly looked at me tenderly.

"Like I told you two years ago, Hugh, you planted them far too deeply. The poor things must have given up struggling to get through, if they ever germinated at all."

"Wasn't Bob pleased with his lettuces, though!"

We both smiled at the memory of Bob's surprise when he came home and saw his flourishing row of lettuces.

Good old Bob. He had tactfully refused our invitation to this anniversary meal, but was joining us later for a drink at the pub.

"It's a good job I threw that seed packet away." Kelly leaned against me. "Those seedlings you got weren't Cos like the ones on the packet, you know. They were curly ones."

"I never realised that. Thought the wind had blown the packet away."

Gently I put my arms round Kelly and the query twins.

"I was pretty green in those days, wasn't I?"

Kelly twirled a strand of my hair round her finger.

"Green as a lettuce," she answered.

——————— * **THE END** * ———————

Complete
Story By
PAMELA
SPECK

"It's My Life To Live"

They never dreamed a child of theirs would do such a thing. But that was the whole problem — she wasn't a child, she was a young woman . . .

IT was exactly like the last time, Judith Ross thought muzzily, lying on the hard, high bed. There was the same strong smell of antiseptic and the loud *tick-tick-tick* of the delivery-room clock. Even the white-coated figures murmuring in the background seemed the same.

She closed her eyes. Gradually her senses began to clear and she could hear what it was that the nurses were murmuring. And she knew then that nothing was really the same — it wasn't like the last time at all . . .

"At her age . . ." she heard.

"All sorts of risks involved . . ."

"Such a pity about the baby."

So she had lost him, she thought dully. She didn't know how she knew it had been a boy, but there wasn't any doubt in her mind. The son she had longed for, the baby who was going to make them a family again — stillborn.

The tears slid slowly from under her closed eyelids, and she felt she could never be bothered to open them again.

They must have been watching her, for a hand mopped her face with a cool cloth and she heard a nurse's voice say, "There now, Mrs Ross."

Then somebody else, trying to be kind, added, "It isn't as though you haven't already got your family. They'll be a comfort to you now, you know."

Oh no, she thought, don't let them talk about my family. Anything but that, make them *stop* . . . for they were wrong.

She didn't have a family, not any more. Not since Linda had left home that night closing the door so quietly behind her. Her daughter, Linda, who had brought so many hopes and dreams with her when she was born, in this very hospital. It seemed like only yesterday . . .

Despair flooded over her, and she threw her arm across her face and sobbed.

T HE nurse's voice was firmer now.

"It's time you got tidied up, Mrs Ross. Your husband will be along in a moment. You don't want him to see you like this. It's his loss, too —just think how he'll feel if he sees you like this."

After a moment, Judith allowed herself to be propped up on the pillows and have a pretty nightdress put on. Then she gave her hair a few dutiful strokes with the brush someone handed her. She was relieved that she was in a side ward, and not in the main maternity ward. She couldn't have borne to be among those young mothers with their new babies, remembering how it had been when Linda was born . . .

★   ★   ★   ★

"She looks just like you," Phil had said softly, when he'd come back from the nursery. He'd been gone a long time and Judith had been picturing him gazing at their new daughter's tiny face, just as she had done.

Would they ever get over the wonder of their child, she had wondered blissfully.

She had lain awake at nights, listening to the sounds from the nearby nursery, dreaming of the things her daughter would do. Maybe she'd be a dancer, or a school teacher. Perhaps a nurse, like the cheerful young women who ran the ward.

And in the darkness, she had smiled at her dreams, knowing they were the same ones every new baby brings.

It never occurred to her, lulled by the hopes of new motherhood, that things might turn out differently.

And even as the years had passed, she had never imagined that there would come a time when she'd despair of those dreams. But come it had on the night she had gone home and found eighteen-year-old Linda and her father in the middle of a fierce argument.

Even now it hurt to remember that scene. At first, she hadn't been able to believe it was her daughter's voice. After all, Linda was supposed to be at teacher-training college, more than a hundred miles away. And surely, she'd thought, that couldn't be Phil, shouting at his adored daugther?

B UT it *was;* Linda and Phil — red-faced and furious, confronting each other across the kitchen table. They fell silent when Judith stepped into the room.

She stared at them, bewildered for a moment.

"Linda — what are you doing home? Are you all right?"

But Linda brushed aside her concern.

"I'm all right, Mother," she said briefly. And it was left to Phil to answer the question.

"What's she doing home!" he put in grimly. "You may well ask! She's packed in college and come back here — *that's* what she's doing home!"

Judith turned to her daughter, aghast. Linda was only in her first year at college and had seemed to be getting on so well. She had seemed a little unsettled, admittedly, but settling took time. It was what they had always wanted for her, and she had worked so hard to get there.

"Linda, what's wrong?" she asked. "It's not true?"

Say it isn't true, she prayed, say you aren't just throwing those years of work and all our hopes down the drain. Anxiety laced itself into her thoughts — all sorts of strange things seemed to happen to perfectly normal children when they started dropping out of college . . .

Linda nodded. "It's true, Mum," she replied quietly.

She had gone very pale, and Judith realised that whatever had brought it on, this decision had been building up for weeks, if not months. It must have taken all the girl's courage to do what she'd done.

She wished desperately that she'd been at home when Linda arrived instead of Phil. Arguments and recriminations weren't called for. What the girl needed was love and understanding and a hot cup of tea. Exactly what she herself needed, she thought wearily, after her visit to the doctor's surgery . . .

But tea and sympathy was obviously the last thing either of them was going to get. Phil had always been hot tempered and hasty — as much as she loved him, Judith had to admit that.

Now, his temper was at its worst, and she knew from past experience that there would be no stopping him. She gave a small sigh and eased herself into a chair. This would have to happen, tonight of all nights, when she was going to tell him about the baby. As if one shock for the family wasn't enough!

"Do you realise what your mother and I have gone through to get you to college?" Phil was demanding.

"Oh, Dad," Linda said wearily, "I *know* all that. But can *you* imagine what I've been through to come to this decision? Look, all I want to do is take a bit of time to think, to sort myself out —"

"Sort yourself out!" Phil's voice was scornful. "That's all you kids want to do nowadays!"

Linda had lost her temper then.

"Oh, for Pete's sake, can't you just be quiet for a moment and let me talk!" she snapped. "You've done nothing but go on and on at me from the moment I walked through the door! Hasn't it occurred to you that *I* might possibly have something to say, too!"

"*Linda!*" Judith interrupted quickly. "Whatever it is you've got to say don't say it in that tone of voice! There's no need to be rude to either of us!"

Linda shrugged tiredly. And for the first time, Judith noticed the girl still had her coat on . . .

If only I'd been at home, she thought again, only this time with a feeling of panic. For Linda was picking up her duffel bag and heading, not for the stairs — but for the door.

Suddenly, Judith remembered the car she'd seen parked outside, with its sidelights on. And how the girl inside had turned her head away when she'd drawn close.

Judith had paid no notice then, but it was obvious now — the car had been waiting for her daughter. Linda must have known she wouldn't be given the chance to explain — and made arrangements to leave . . .

"Where are you going, Linda?" Judith asked, surprised at the steadiness of her own voice.

Linda dropped a kiss on her head.

"Just away, for a while, Mum," she replied. "I've got to think things out for myself. I've quit college for good, I'm not going back. Honestly, I don't see any point in spending years of my life studying to do something I don't want to do."

"But, darling. I thought you always wanted to teach —"

"No, Mum!" Linda's voice was firm. "It was you and Dad who always wanted me to teach. I went along with what you wanted because I had no idea what *I* wanted. Now, I think it's time I found out."

She was gone then, swiftly, before either of them could say anything else, the door closing quietly behind her.

It was hours later that Judith, lying sleepless in the dark, remembered that Linda hadn't said where she was going, or for how long.

And she herself hadn't told Phil about the baby . . .

YOU'RE sure you're going to be all right?" Phil asked with concern, when she told him the next day.

Judith knew he was remembering Linda's birth, and how difficult it had been for her, but there was nothing she could say to put his mind at rest. After all, even her doctor, when he had confirmed her pregnancy, had had doubts he had voiced plainly.

But she wasn't going to be put off and discouraged — they had said almost the same things when she was having Linda.

"There are always risks with someone my age," she told Phil, then smiled. "I'm not a brand-new mother, you know!"

He took her in his arms then.

"I'm sorry I got so angry with Linda last night, love," he said. "I just hope it hasn't upset you too much. If only she had known, perhaps she would have been a bit more reasonable."

Judith didn't reply. She couldn't bring herself to tell him he'd been unreasonable himself. He'd see that in time, he always did.

"Where do you suppose she's gone?" she asked anxiously. It had been worrying her all night.

"Oh, she'll be all right," Phil said optimistically. "Probably at her Aunt Ella's."

Ella, Phil's sister, was only a few years older than Linda herself, and had a flat in the city. Linda had often spent weekends there. There was nothing to worry about, Judith kept telling herself. Besides her aunt's, there were any number of places she could have gone, for she was a popular girl with a great many friends . . .

"She'll call soon," Phil said, still hearty. "She'll be home as soon as she hears your news. You'll see, she'll be as pleased as Punch, just as I am."

But the passing days had turned into weeks, and there was no indication of Linda's whereabouts. The occasional letter came, saying she was well and not to worry, but giving no address.

"Phil, how are we going to get in touch with her?" Judith pleaded. She had never envisaged a situation like this. Supposing the time came for the baby to be born and Linda still wasn't here? Anything could happen — something could go wrong . . . Linda would never forgive herself.

They *had* to let her know, somehow.

But Phil's face showed defeat.

"She's over eighteen," he said helplessly. "And we do hear from her, so she isn't exactly what you might call a missing person. I don't see what we can do."

Continued on page 126

SLIM first came into our lives several years ago. My husband and I were settling down to a quiet life, after a visit from friends, but our "find" was soon to change that!

Our next-door neighbour was busy turning out his garage. He threw out a nest he found there, and when we examined it curiously, we discovered a tiny baby animal inside. Its mother must have fled, terrified, when she heard all the noise. Even though it had no fur, my husband realised it must be a weasel.

It was such a shame to think it would die, that we decided to try our hardest to see what we could do to keep it alive.

We carried the poor creature indoors, where we prepared a small box, lining it with cotton wool. Gently we laid him down, noticing as we did so that his eyes were tightly closed. That meant he could only be a few days old.

Next we warmed some milk. His mouth was so small that we wondered how we could feed him, but we found a compass pen which held the correct amount and proved the best idea.

Gently, he lapped the milk from it and we felt so happy to think we had achieved something. We fed him every three hours, which meant getting up throughout the night.

There was also a problem created by the fact we were both out working all day. My husband solved this by taking the tiny animal to work with him in the car, complete with hot-water bottle and warm milk in a vacuum flask. He did this every day for about a month.

We got some information about weasels and discovered they don't open their eyes for about 10 weeks.

Every day we would look at h and wonder if he would surviv that long.

From time to time, he wou show signs of life. Sometimes would whimper, especially if bed was dirty or the water bo we kept under him all the time w losing its heat and he was getti cold.

Then one day we noticed sor down on his face. It was very so Also, he could move around a lit by now, so we thought he shou have another box with separa sleeping quarters.

I bought some hamster beddi and he loved it. Every night would block up the doorway fre the inside so he couldn't be see Then he would make his own b with a little hole in the centr where he would curl up into a b and go to sleep.

AS the weeks passed, v introduced egg yolk to milk in the little creature's die thinking it would make a chan for him. He liked it very much a sometimes refused plain milk.

SLIM

When we first found him, was so tiny, it seemed imp sible for Slim to survive. I as I, his "foster mother," so discovered, there was a more to this scrap of life th met the eyes . . .

My husband started bathing him every day, but he hated that. Sometimes he would wriggle free, and we'd have a job to catch him.

One day he tried to dry himself by rubbing himself right along the carpet. Other times he would climb on to my husband's shoulder and dry himself on his pullover.

He was really winning us over with his antics and becoming one of the family, so we thought it was time he had a name. As the little animal's body was getting so long, my husband suggested Slim. It suited him, so it stayed.

The next landmark in Slim's life was when one of his eyes opened, one weekend. We were really excited, and then a few days later the other one opened, too. They were dark brown and very bright.

Goodness knows what will happen now he can see, we thought, he'll be into everything!

Slim was growing fast now and his coat was very beautiful. It was a rich brown, and so shiny, and he had a pure white underbelly.

We had read that weasels kill to eat and have lots of courage, so we thought we might have to watch our step if we didn't want to lose a finger when he grew up!

Now that he could see, Slim became much more playful. One day we put a plastic egg-cup in his box.

Talk about a stage show! He threw it around, rolled with it, then finally carried it into his bedroom. We enjoyed watching him and wouldn't have believed he could be so entertaining if we hadn't seen him with our own eyes.

One evening we decided he should have a play-pen. My husband rigged one up. It was made of wood, and about three feet high. He wouldn't be able to get out of that, we told ourselves happily.

Carefully, we placed him inside the pen and in no time at all he had climbed up the side and

Our little
Bundle
of joy

By
Stella
Burrows

121

jumped. He was free. Round and round the lounge he ran, enjoying himself immensely. We couldn't catch him for quite some time, but when we finally managed to, he went straight to his bed, tired out, and stayed there for ages.

We decided to try again. Another box was made, also of wood. This one had an upstairs and downstairs, ramps to run up and down, and a special place for his food. He didn't like that part of the arrangements, though, and decided to use it as a toilet!

We put this house in a spare room, where every evening we went to play with him. Goodness knows how many somersaults he turned, it was impossible to count them. We really enjoyed being with him, he had so much energy. And it was touching, the way he trusted us. Not once did he attempt to bite us, but nibbled our fingers in play.

EVERY night during the winter, Slim slept in the smaller box, which was cosier. We would fetch him from the spare room, and he knew exactly what this meant. He would climb on to our shoulders and stay there until we reached the lounge. Then he scrambled down our arm and straight into bed, to make his nest and have a long sleep.

As he grew, we weaned Slim with raw meat, which we chopped up very finely. He could only take a little at first, but gradually the amount increased.

He still loved his egg and milk at suppertime, though. Once we tried to give him boiled egg yolk and some cereal with warm milk for a change, but he soon told us what to do with that! The egg was thrown into the corner, and the cereal scattered everywhere.

He was endearingly funny, and

had us just where he wanted us.

There were other variations in Slim's life, and travelling was one of them.

We spent every Christmas with my husband's family in Kent. Of course, if we went this time, Slim would have to go, too, and that is just what happened. A lot of organising had to be done, but we were so fond of Slim we didn't mind the extra bother at all.

In the end, Sandy, our dog, sat on the back seat of the car with Slim beside him, tucked up in his box. He really seemed to enjoy the journey. I don't believe Sandy knew who was sitting beside him, so it all went off without a hitch.

When we arrived, everyone made a fuss of Slim, especially Martin, a nephew of ours. He was very keen to take his photograph. My husband opened the front of the box, and in a flash Slim ran straight over his hand and dug his teeth into Martin's hand.

It must have hurt really badly, and of course Martin cried out in pain, but afterwards he said to Slim, "I still think you are gorgeous!"

The incident taught us a lesson, though — not to let strangers near him again.

It was on another visit we made to Kent that we nearly lost Slim. Slim was living in my mother-in-law's garage, and my husband was giving him his supper there. Slim managed to escape from his box and went rummaging around in all the firewood, garden tools and all the other things that accumulate in garages.

We couldn't find him for hours and began to think that perhaps he had gone altogether. By this time, obviously, Slim must have been bewildered and frightened.

I sat on the floor and listened for

a long time, then I heard a faint scratch. We moved some wood and there he was, covered in cobwebs and looking so dejected and miserable. I felt so sorry for the poor little thing I just had to cry.

Well, Slim soon went back into his box. You would have thought he had been fired out of a gun by the speed he travelled! I don't suppose he will do that again, and I certainly hope not — it was one o'clock in the morning when that episode finished!

SPRING came the year after we found Slim. He was almost fully grown now. Many times we wondered whether we should release him, and if we did, whether he would be able to fend for himself in the wild. We couldn't teach him to hunt as his mother would have, and kill for his food. Also, we weren't sure whether the other weasels would accept him now.

It was a big decision to make. We wanted to do what was best for Slim. So, after a great deal of discussion, we decided he would never be able to cope on his own.

Now that we had decided this, the next task was to build him a permanent home outside. My husband designed and built it to give Slim every comfort. It was big enough to give him plenty of room to roam around, and there were

two doors to make easier entry for us. His sleeping quarters were very private, as Slim loves to have somewhere to hide. And the thing he likes most of all is his bed, which he keeps spotless and he makes so beautifully.

At last Slim's new home was ready, and no-one could have been happier than Slim when we introduced him to it. He was terribly excited and ran around, exploring every inch of it, almost, it seemed, as if to see whether it was suitable. It was a real joy to see him so happy, and we knew we had done the right thing.

There was every comfort in his new home, a heater under his bedroom, and an infra-red lamp for when it was really cold. He even had a playroom with lots of toys: a slipper, a piece of fur, a ball and numerous other things, all of which he loved.

Every night we would spend a quarter of an hour or so with him, which we thoroughly enjoyed. He is such a delightful animal, and so clever, too.

Many times we have laughed at him. One of his habits that amuses us is when we take his food in to him and then start to close the door, he comes chasing at us, as much as to say, "Go away while I'm eating."

It is over two years now since we began caring for Slim. It's been a lot of hard work, but we can say now with all honesty it has been well worth every minute of it. He has more than repaid us by being so friendly and sweet.

However long Slim lives, we will do our utmost to make him happy, and afterwards treasure some wonderful memories of a dear little weasel who, thanks to a lucky accident, did have a life and enjoyed it so much after all. ■

" And "
I Quote ...

JOHN CLEESE (1939), actor and writer, educated at Cambridge, was a prominent member of the TV show "Monty Python's Flying Circus" (1969-74). He was later co-author with Connie Booth (his first wife, and actress in the series) of "Fawlty Towers," and scriptwriter and director of the film "A Fish Called Wanda."

When I asked you to build me a wall I was rather hoping that instead of just dumping the bricks in a pile you might have found time to cement them together.

She can kill a man at 10 paces with one blow of her tongue.

Have you seen the people in Room Six? They've never even sat on chairs before.

BASIL. I fought in the Korean War, you know. I killed four men . . .
SYBIL. He was in the catering corps. He poisoned them.

" And "
I Quote ...

DENIS NORDEN (1922), humorous script writer, born in London, has his own brand of dry wit. He achieved success on radio, with Frank Muir, with *Take It From Here* (1948-60), and has since presented many series on radio and TV both with Muir and solo.

" And "
I Quote ...

LES DAWSON (1934) was born in Manchester. After surviving poverty and a variety of jobs he became a popular TV comedian, at one time with his own show *Sez Les*. *A Clown Too Many*(1985) is his autobiography.

When she lightly kissed me upon my cheek, it felt as though I had been savaged by a frankfurter.

The money meant luxuries such as food and shoes.

"I have been discharged from the [Mental] Institution" [she wrote] "and I'm back at my old job in a solicitor's office. I work there as a teapot."

I used to sell furniture for a living. The trouble was, it was my own.

The neighbours love it when I play the piano. They break my window to hear me better.

He had the kind of handshake that ought never to be used except as a tourniquet.

What is a harp but an over-sized cheese-slicer with cultural pretensions.

When giving children's parties, never serve eight jugs of orangeade in a house which has only one bathroom.

If I were asked to enumerate the Seven Deadly Virtues, the one I'd put right at the top of my list is Female Tidiness.

She had him standing for two hours trying to straighten a watercolour of the Leaning Tower of Pisa.

There is an unseen force which lets birds know when you've just washed your car.

A counter tenor is anyone who can count to ten.

Continued from page 119
Judith didn't reply. She knew all too clearly all they could do was wait, and hope . . .

NOW in her tidy hospital bed, Judith wept again — for the baby she had lost, for herself, and for Linda, who never had come back . . .

Firm arms came around her, and Phil's voice said, "No more tears now, darling, please."

"Oh, Phil, the baby . . ." she sobbed.

He held her closer. "I know, Judith, I know."

Now it was all over. Her pregnancy had passed, her baby had been born and died — and Linda had known nothing. She raised her tear-stained face. She had to ask.

"Linda — ?"

Phil shook his head, his face grim.

"It's my fault, Judith," he said. "I shouldn't have been so pig-headed, I should have listened to what she had to say. She needed my understanding and all I did was shout at her. All I could think of was the plans we had for her, and the money we'd spent."

Judith touched his hand gently.

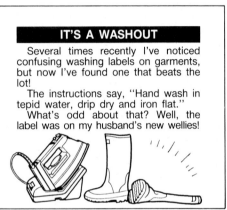

IT'S A WASHOUT

Several times recently I've noticed confusing washing labels on garments, but now I've found one that beats the lot!

The instructions say, "Hand wash in tepid water, drip dry and iron flat."

What's odd about that? Well, the label was on my husband's new wellies!

"You couldn't help it, Phil. Neither of us knew how she felt about teaching, we really thought she wanted to. It's far better for her to have given up when she did, anyway, rather than later. We — we didn't know — that was all. She'll be back in her own time."

Judith hoped her voice was as convincing as her words.

Somehow, the days in the hospital went by. Each letter that arrived she opened eagerly, each visiting hour she said a small prayer . . . the next time the doors open, let it be her. But Phil's face gave her the same answer every day. There had been nothing from Linda.

After a while, she was able to walk in the main maternity ward, to stop and chat with the new mothers. They, above all, who held their babies so close and warm, knew how she was feeling.

It was the nights she couldn't bear. The sounds of the nursery reached her then, even in the side ward; but this time she didn't smile in the dark . . .

"Nearly time to go home!" one of the nurses said to her cheerfully one day.

Judith managed to return her smile. She longed to get back and lead a normal life again, yet in a way she dreaded actually leaving.

It was the walk from the ward to the car she dreaded most, remembering how it had been the last time. Then, she had taken her daughter, and her dreams. Now, she would take nothing. Her arms would be empty, her hopes all faded.

"I'll come early and fetch you," Phil said. He must have known what she was thinking. It would be almost the same for him, too.

IT must be over and done with as soon as possible, Judith thought, packing her case. I mustn't be silly about this, I'm a grown woman, and I knew almost from the start there was every chance it would happen.

She was dressed and waiting to leave when the telephone call came. It was Phil.

"Judith? Listen, love, I'm sorry, but I've been held up. There's the most awful traffic jam on the motorway and I've only just managed to get to a phone and call you."

Judith's heart sank. This journey home was going to be bad enough — but without Phil beside her, it would be unbearable.

"I'll get a taxi, Phil," she said, trying to sound brisk and in control. But he broke in firmly.

"No, don't do that, love. You're not to go home by yourself. Just wait there. I'll get to you as soon as I can. Look, I must go now. Wait for me, all right?"

The line went dead, and Judith put down the receiver. She went back to her bed, already re-made for the next occupant, and sat on the chair beside it.

It was natural to feel weak and emotional, she knew. But she mustn't give in, she must pull herself together.

When Phil came she must walk through that ward, bright with flowers and smiling faces, and not think about how it might have been if her own baby had lived. Not think about the empty house she was returning to, the cold fireplace, Linda's room so neat and tidy — and unused . . .

She leaned her head back and closed her eyes. She didn't want to think about any of it, she didn't want to think at all . . .

After a time, the door opened softly and footsteps came towards her. That would be one of the nurses, perhaps coming to tell her that Phil was here.

She opened her eyes — and stared. She hadn't known it was possible for the world to change from grey to glorious brightness in a single second.

"Linda!"

She felt soft arms around her, a cheek against her own, a voice she hadn't heard for months whispered, "Mother — Mother, forgive me!"

They held each other close.

"Darling, where have you been? We've missed you so, wanted to tell you —"

"Oh, Mum. I'm sorry, I'm sorry." Linda's words tumbled out. "I thought it would be all right if I dropped you a line now and then to to tell you I was fine — I never dreamed you'd have anything like this to tell me!"

Her young face was full of remorse.

"Oh, Mum, I could kick myself for walking out like that, at that time, too. All I could think about was myself and how mixed up I was. If only I'd been home to help, this might never have happened!"

Judith shook her head.

"No, Linda, you mustn't think that. It would have happened in any case — we must accept that. Really, I think I knew from the beginning . . ."

She paused. "But how are you, love?" She smiled through her tears. "Your father's never forgiven himself for not listening to you. We've been so worried, wondering about you, what you've decided to do —"

"That's what I came home to tell you. I rang Aunt Ella, you see. I — I wanted to know if she'd heard from you or Dad. I could have died when she told me what had happened. I came right away. Oh, Mum, I feel so ashamed . . ."

Judith interrupted gently. "Stop that now. Your father and I were just as much to blame. We shouldn't have pushed you into teacher's training. And I — I should have made him listen to you that night." She paused. "Have you thought about your future, Linda?"

Her daughter nodded. "That's what I've got to tell you. I've been accepted for training as a children's nurse. It's always been in the back of my mind, but it sounded so unambitious — and you and Dad always had such plans for me, it — it seemed like letting you down.

"But I've decided to go ahead with it, and I'm starting next month, not very far from home either."

She looked up anxiously, waiting for approval.

Heaven forgive us, Judith thought suddenly, for wanting to live Linda's life for her. Then she smiled.

A children's nurse, she thought, so there were going to be babies around after all. Lots and lots of babies!

"I think that's wonderful!" she said. "And I'm dying to hear all about it. Let's go home and have a cup of tea together, and you can fill me in on all the details . . ."

Then as she stood up, she noticed there was someone else in the room, standing silently by the door.

"Phil . . ." she whispered, and tears mounted in her eyes as she watched Linda run into his arms.

Yes, she thought, I'm ready to leave now.

For once again she was going with her husband and daughter — and her dreams, which she thought had faded, were even brighter then they had been those years and years ago.

——————— * **THE END** * ———————

All In The Game . . .

"ALL I own in the world is a bed, a shed and a silver condiment set!"

That statement was intended as a conversation stopper and, believe me, it was effective.

A deathly silence fell over the small gathering of friends I'd invited over for the evening. Every head turned to the speaker.

No, he wasn't down-at-the-heel or shabbily dressed. He was, I knew, a very successful businessman. I also knew that he meant what he said.

I glanced with a knowing smile at his long-suffering wife. She winked.

"It's true," she said. "Tell them about it, dear."

She needn't have bothered. He had no intention of doing anything else.

I had heard his story before. It never failed to amuse me — or amaze me that he could tell it without the merest hint of a smile.

Years ago, as a young husband, he repeatedly made a very simple mistake. He kept referring to *his* house, *his* living-room carpet, *his* garden.

His young wife duly corrected him and pointed out they were "our possessions."

But she did it once too often and too forcefully. With great dignity and due ceremony, he officially signed over everything to her. Everything, that is, but the bed. That, he insisted, was his.

Some years later he acquired a garden shed. That was his! He checked that *his* bed would go in it, just in case he was ever thrown out of the house.

The only other thing he acquired over the years was a silver condiment set. How, no-one can remember. Still, who would grudge him it?

Certainly not his wife, who goes along with his game.

And so, you see, he's right. All he has in the world are a bed, a shed and a silver condiment set.

Oh, yes — and a very happy marriage!

Calamity BEN

Clumsy at work, hopeless at hobbies, was it any real surprise that when it came to romance he had to fall for the wrong girl?

BENJAMIN HARDY never had much of a voice. He would lie in the bath, and sing what he thought were powerful solos until he was red in the face, while the dog, down below in the kitchen, would promptly lift his head and howl.

"Out of tune, Benjy!" his mother would shout up, but Benjy would simmer quietly — and silently dream of becoming a world-famous tenor, or even more fantastically, a pop star.

Until that happened Benjy went on working in the estate agents' office he had joined on leaving school a few months ago. And it was while he was there that he first saw Jackie. He'd never seen anyone so perfect and he began opening and shutting doors for clients, in the hope of catching a glimpse of her at work in the boutique across the road.

One old lady mentioned Benjy's "olde-worlde" courtesy to Mr Higgins, the senior partner, who blinked in surprise as Benjy roared off down the High Street on his orange scooter, revving the engine for Jackie's benefit.

So far, though, Benjy hadn't actually met Jackie.

He wanted his sister, Patsy, who also worked in the boutique, to introduce them, but she was adamant.

"You'll only take her out a couple of times then drop her. Like you did to Priscilla and Mary and Edna." She reeled off the names of her friends in the boutique and Benjy flushed.

"But this time it's different," he said, really meaning it. Like he always did.

Continued on page 132

Complete Story By BARBARA DUFFIELD

131

"It always is," she replied tartly, "till the next one. Anyway, she's not your type."

"What do you mean, my type?" he demanded.

Patsy shrugged. "Oh, discos, late-night films. She's different, that's all."

"How *different*?"

"Well . . ." She thought for a second.

"She's joining the operatic society, for a start."

"She is?" He grinned. "But I like opera. I know *Madam Butterfly* and *Carmen* and . . ." He ran out of inspiration and ducked as Patsy threw a cushion at him.

"Of course," she told him sweetly, "you could always join the society yourself if you really want to meet her."

Benjy gazed at his face in a mirror. Well, why not join? That would show them. Always shouting at him about his voice. He'd be in the chorus, and stride about dressed as a Foreign Legionnaire, or cavalier, and bowl Jackie off her feet into the bargain.

But when he applied he was told they only had a vacancy for a scene shifter.

"Scene shifter? *Me?*" His voice rose to a squeak.

"Sorry, Benjamin," the secretary said firmly. "We're always short of people backstage. You know, it's very important. We couldn't even put on a production without the scene shifters and the wardrobe people. I'm sure you'd enjoy it."

He stared at her, still pink from the rebuff. He knew he was no Caruso, but not even to be in the chorus . . .

He thought of what Patsy would say if he told her.

Then he saw Jackie, over by the stage, laughing with a group of people. Her eyes met his and he was sunk. He needn't tell anyone what he did, after all, and he *was* a member of the society . . .

"OK, I'll do scene shifting," he said gruffly.

It was very difficult even to meet Jackie, though. She was always prancing around with the chorus, a crowd of giggling girls, and he was constantly busy helping to paint and make scenery, as well as shift it.

They rehearsed in a draughty old hall that was so chilly the girls wore heavy sweaters despite the watery autumn sunshine outside.

It was all made much worse by a girl who thought she knew everything.

Benjy took an instant dislike to her. She was the sort of girl who made him prickle with antagonism.

"You must be the new backstage helper. Well, I'm Angie," she introduced herself.

She was about his age and stared at him through wide, horn-rimmed glasses. She was almost as tall as he was, and her hair was tied in a long plait. She had a smudge of dust on one cheek and wore faded jeans covered in paint splodges.

She was just about the most unfeminine girl he'd ever seen — not a bit like Jackie.

"Yes," he admitted and winced as she thrust a large piece of hardboard at him.

"Can you make a cut-out of a palm tree to go in this corner?"

Benjy reeled under the onslaught. He'd never made anything in his life except a soap-box car, and that had collapsed on its first outing!

"Oh!" Impatiently she pushed at him a box of tools he didn't recognise. "Here, I'll show you!"

"I can do it!" Benjy snapped. He wasn't going to be shown what to do by this infuriating female. She looked at him over the top of her glasses, and he noticed she had green eyes.

"If you muck it up there'll be trouble," she said shortly. "We haven't got much money to spare on this production."

"I," Benjy told her coldly, "am quite capable of making a palm tree."

He wasn't though. It was lopsided, bent in the middle, and gracefully sagged to the ground when Angie came to inspect it.

He wished that he'd never heard of amateur operatics. He hadn't even met Jackie yet, and here he was making palm trees.

Angie's face was a picture of dismay.

"Oh, really! You said you *could* make it! Just look, it's more like a broken daffodil!"

Benjy scratched his head with the hammer. "Well. It hasn't turned out quite the way I expected," he confessed lamely.

"You'll be stuck with the scene shifters if you don't watch out," she said grimly.

At that moment Jackie pranced past them, dressed as a harem girl. Benjy approved the choice of rôle. His eyes followed her until Angie Thompson jerked him back to earth.

"Are you going to concentrate on this palm tree or not?"

FROM that moment Angie Thompson became the bane of his life. Whenever he found a quiet corner so he could gaze adoringly at Jackie, she would give him jobs.

Even so, he watched Jackie singing, and he watched her dancing. But so far all he'd done was queue up for her coffee twice and walk home with her once. And then there had been three others with them, and one of those had been Angie.

He'd tried to stay by Jackie's side, but Dave Prentis, who had an embryo beard, stuck to her like a leech. And as Angie was on the other side, so Benjy was stuck next to Angie.

She strode along like a boy, hands stuck in duffel coat pockets. Jackie had asked Angie what she did.

"I'm at art school," she'd replied, and she'd sounded diffident, so unlike the Angie who'd ordered him around at rehearsals.

"You are? Oh, clever you!" Jackie had exclaimed. "What are you going to be?"

Angie had hesitated then. "Well — I'd like to do fashion design. But I'm taking a general course now. I like stage work, though. I'd rather like to do costumes for the shows."

Benjy had snorted silently. Angie Thompson, who lived in jeans and painty sweaters, doing fashion design? He might have known she was something arty, though. She had that sort of dedicated air people get when they're keen on poetry or painting.

He tried to jostle her across the pavement so he could get closer to Jackie, but she resisted, almost as though she knew what he was trying to do.

"Er, Jackie," he'd blurted out, "how about a coffee in the Sugar Plum?" It was a favourite haunt of his.

"Oh, I can't. Thanks all the same." She'd smiled at him over the collar of her bright red cape. "Why don't you take Angie, though? I'm sure she'd like it."

Angie had replied with almost insulting haste, "Sorry, no. I have to get home. I've some studying to do."

Benjy shrugged and was left to walk home alone in the soft harvest moonlight, dreaming of Jackie and the day when she'd agree to come out with him. She would, he was sure.

She'd have to, or he'd never be happy again.

Somehow, though, he was always stuck with Angie and the scenery at rehearsals, and Jackie remained a distant enchantment.

Angie had begun bringing a flask of hot chocolate and one evening grudgingly offered it to him. He'd forgotten to bring a sweater and felt chilly.

"Here," she said. "You'd better have a drink before you freeze to death."

They sat on upturned boxes and watched the hero singing his solo.

Benjy eyed him wistfully, wishing he could sing like that, instead of being out of tune all the time. He turned to hand Angie the flask and surprised an odd look on her face.

"Hey!" He spoke without thinking. "Can't you sing, either?"

She flushed. "It always comes out flat. Anyway," she shook the long plait behind her back, "more fun backstage."

"Fun!" Benjy surveyed his blackened thumb where he'd thumped it with a hammer and the large splinter sticking in his little finger. For a moment he realised Angie had been almost human, as if she had some dreams of her own.

"Come on!" She got up and began being busy. "Got to get this door fixed. Give me a hand, Benjy."

Reluctantly, he went to help.

She was always ordering him about, as though he didn't know anything. Though, come to think of it, he didn't know much about stage carpentry — or want to, for that matter. Though he had to admit she seemed to know what she was doing. She even told the older people how to work, and she was, oddly enough, popular with everyone — except Benjy.

However, after that, she brought her flask to all the rehearsals and he found himself looking forward to the snatched 10 minutes behind scenes.

Then they began the painting and she was worse than ever. It was,

"Paint this, mix that, try that colour, fetch the bucket over, we want some more whitewash . . ."

Benjy realised it was harder work than his job with the estate agents, and at least he got paid for that!

Then the miracle happened.

HE was leaving the hall early one night, when there was Jackie, standing on the step alone for once. Fingers crossed, he asked her for a date.

"Well," she looked him over dubiously, "coffee after the next rehearsal?"

For the next two days he walked on air and waved to her from the estate agent as she did the window-dressing in the boutique across the road. He bought a new shirt, and resolutely decided not to cover it up with a sweater — even if he caught pneumonia.

Then he put his foot in it.

There he was, putting the finishing touches to a set, wielding a large dripping paintbrush full of sky-blue paint, when Jackie came running round the back of the stage.

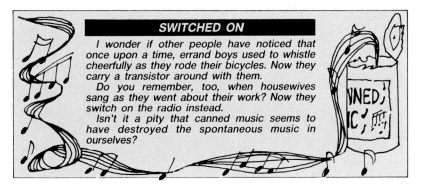

SWITCHED ON

I wonder if other people have noticed that once upon a time, errand boys used to whistle cheerfully as they rode their bicycles. Now they carry a transistor around with them.

Do you remember, too, when housewives sang as they went about their work? Now they switch on the radio instead.

Isn't it a pity that canned music seems to have destroyed the spontaneous music in ourselves?

"Jackie! You haven't forgotten, have you?" He leaned down eagerly from the step-ladder . . . and knocked over the tin of paint . . .

Her shriek stopped the chorus in full blast.

"Oh! Benjy! What have you *done*! My new trousers! Oh!"

She stood there with blue paint dripping down the black-and-red check slacks he'd seen in the boutique window only a few days ago. He scrambled down the ladder, and tried to mop up the paint with an old rag.

"Don't! You'll make it worse! Stop! You — you clumsy idiot!"

"I'm sorry! Jackie, I'm terribly sorry!" he stammered at her helplessly.

"Do something!" she wailed.

Then Angie appeared and thrust a rag and a bottle in her hands.

"Turps," she said briefly. "Go in the cloakroom and sponge it off, Jackie. It'll be all right."

She turned to Benjy. "Come on. We want you to give us a hand with the props."

Benjy gazed after Jackie's retreating back and had a nasty feeling she wouldn't come and have coffee with him after all.

He was right. Afterwards, she looked right through him as he waited on the steps, collar turned up to his ears, as she came towards him with a group of the chorus.

"Jackie —" he began. "You said — you'd come and have a coffee with me." Benjy, usually so assured with girls, was stammering. He flushed miserably.

She pulled the hood up over her hair.

"Sorry, Benjy," she said coolly, "I have to go home and change. I've still got paint all over me."

And she was gone, leaving him alone in the chill air.

After that it went from bad to worse. One of the cut-outs he'd made collapsed on stage, and fell on two of the chorus girls.

Angie lost her temper with him.

"If you'd only concentrate on what you're doing," she stormed, "instead of mooning over Jackie all the time!"

"I don't!" he defended himself hotly.

"You do! I've seen you! You work for five minutes and watch her for fifteen! In fact, I've done most of your work up to now and you've never even noticed!"

He gazed at her, astonished. Her glasses had slipped down her nose and her hair come unplaited. It whipped across her shoulders as she turned and he saw it was a heavy old-gold colour, gleaming in the arc lights.

He realised with astonishment that she'd looked different lately — and he'd only just noticed. Then her words jerked him into action.

"You're just jealous!" he jeered. "Just because you're not in the production, and you can't sing or dance, and you're not pretty like Jackie!"

The moment he'd said it, he wished he hadn't, for it wasn't true.

Flushed with anger, standing with her eyes almost level with his, she looked very pretty, and he'd never realised it till now. To his horror, tears spilled into her eyes and she blinked rapidly at him.

"What a — cruel thing to say!"

"Angie — I'm sorry. I didn't mean —" But she'd gone, striding off with a bucket of whitewash, determinedly ignoring him. He stared miserably after her and, again, he wished that he'd never joined the operatic society.

AT the next rehearsal Angie wouldn't speak to him, and Jackie ignored him completely.

Doggedly he painted sets and hammered in odd nails, and Angie sat on her upturned box alone so he had to queue with the others for weak coffee.

And Angie didn't even come to the next rehearsal, which was the

Continued on page 141

No Nessie — What A Monstrous Idea!

I DON'T know about you, but whenever I hear that our old friend the Loch Ness Monster has been sighted again, it brings a spring to my step and a lift to my heart.

Call me frivolous. Call me an incurable romantic, but that little item of news does more for my morale than any improvement in the state of the pound.

Nessie has always had an effect on me. It dates back to a holiday I spent in Inverness as a youngster.

I remember being taken on a bus run along the shores of Loch Ness and eagerly scanning the sparkling waves for any sign of a hump or two.

Over the years I've watched Nessie's career with a mixture of feelings.

I've worried over those expeditions we hear of from time to time, who come from all corners of the world bristling with sonar equipment, telephoto cameras and mini submarines.

I know they mean Nessie no physical harm. All they want is clear documented proof of her existence. But even that would be too much for me.

I've sighed with relief when I've realised our Nessie's far too canny a lass to cavort in front of sophisticated cameras.

She much prefers the passing motorist or the lone fisherman. And so do I.

Couldn't it have been a wave they saw, everyone asks? Or, perhaps, driftwood?

Of course it could. That's how the doubt remains — and with the doubt — the mystery and the magic!

I, for one, have no doubt.

She's there all right, waiting to show herself any time she feels our morale needs a boost.

IF you've always steered clear of auctions because you're afraid a sudden unexpected twitch will land you with a costly mistake, think again. You could be missing great bargains and even greater fun.

I'm not talking about grand places like Sotheby's or Christie's — I'd be worried about twitching there — but about smaller auctions held by local firms all over the country.

By Anne Knowles

Don't expect to pick up Constable for a fiver — eve country auctions are attended b knowledgeable dealers nowaday But you should be able to b interesting and useful items, som times quite cheaply.

Saving money is not the on pleasure, however. It can be enjoyable day out. There are ofte

GOING FOR A SONG

Need a nice little side-tabl for the hall? There's no need to pa a small fortune — try you local auction room

refreshments on sale at the auction rooms and a fascinating collection of people gathered there, from city dealers in velvet-collared overcoats, smoking cigars, to unshaven characters in cloth caps and tattered trousers, as well as amateurs like yourself. There is often much friendly banter, as well as helpful advice and information to be had.

Your first step, though, is to ring the auctioneers listed in the Yellow Pages and ask for a catalogue of a forthcoming sale to give you an idea of the merchandise on offer.

Some firms, even in the provinces, are very upmarket, dealing only in fine antiques. Unless you've been left a fortune, forget these. Go for firms dealing in solid old country furniture or Victorian and Edwardian pieces.

Sales of good-quality modern furniture can also be worthwhile hunting grounds. Under a shabby

exterior there is often a sound piece of furniture, traditionally upholstered with horsehair and coiled springs — much less of a fire hazard than foam — which you can have loose-covered in your choice of fabric at a fraction of the cost of a new chair or sofa of similar quality.

Most auctioneers have a viewing day prior to the auction and also for a few hours on the day itself. You are able to look around and examine items much more freely than in a second-hand or antique shop.

You can take out drawers, tap furniture to check for wood-worm, look closely at pottery for cracks. If an article is marked AF in the catalogue, this means As Found and is usually an indication that a piece is fairly obviously damaged.

Watch the bidding on one or two occasions before entering the fray yourself. You will see the pace of the auctioneer — and a good one can clear 50 lots an hour — how the bidding is carried out and whether the prices are in a range that suits you.

ONE day you will be ready to buy. Tick the items you like in your catalogue. Alongside, mark the maximum price you intend to pay, and allow yourself one bid over.

Here's why: you and your opponent will make alternate bids. It may be that the pattern of the bids is such that it is your opponent's turn to bid just when your maximum figure is reached.

This is known as being "on the wrong side of the bid." So allow yourself one bid, and only one, over your maximum.

Until you are very experienced, be very firm with yourself about this. There's no doubt about it, bidding is exciting and it's easy to get carried away.

Making a bid is simple — and contrary to popular belief it's most unlikely that a mistimed blink or sneeze will mean you've bought a 10-foot wardrobe painted purple. There is no prescribed method, but the following technique makes your intentions perfectly clear.

Look directly at the auctioneer, raise your catalogue and nod firmly to indicate yes. Lower your catalogue and shake your head to indicate no. Auctioneers are experienced. They rarely mistake a bid.

If there is any confusion or dispute, simply make it clear immediately and the item will be reauctioned on the spot. I have seen this happen only once in many years of auction going.

If an item is "knocked down" (sold) to you, the auctioneer will ask for your name. This will be transferred, with details of your purchase, to a clerk who sits in the sale room or in an office nearby.

You are expected to pay for your goods before the end of the sale and to clear all items promptly. Remember this if you are hoping to buy furniture, and take a roof rack or make an allowance for the cost of transport home in your bidding price. Porters (for a small tip) and other buyers are usually happy to help you manhandle the stuff on to your car.

AS you get more exprienced, take an interest in the other merchandise, too, and while away the time waiting for your lot to come up by estimating how much you think an item will make and seeing how close you get.

This worked to my advantage one day, several years ago, when a pretty, walnut side-table which I had estimated would sell for about £90 — 'way beyond my pocket then — was about to be knocked down for £15. Immediately, I came in with a bid of £1 more and the table was knocked down to me for £16. Its mellow glow increases with the years and has given me continuing pleasure.

Many auction purchases just need a good clean or polish to transform them. Remember, though, if you buy, for example, a damaged antique or a Victorian chair frame, the cost of skilled labour to restore it could make it an expensive purchase in the long run.

But there are many potentially attractive items — tables, chairs and chests — which simply need a new handle or perhaps stripping and varnishing. Most people can manage these straightforward, if tedious tasks. There are many helpful books available and DIY shops sell strippers, oils and restoring materials with very clear instructions which produce excellent results even for a beginner.

It's fun to take your treasures home — a pretty chair for the hall, a picture, some blue and white pottery to add to your collection — all with an associated memory. You will recall the pleasure of buying an attractive vase for less than you expected, the character in eccentric clothes who bid against you for the enamelled box, or the January day you nearly froze to death in a barn-like auction room, but came home triumphant with a pretty work-table. The thrill of the chase never fades.

There's a space on my dining-room wall at the moment — just the place for that Constable I might get for a fiver one day! ∎

Continued from page 136

first dress rehearsal. Foreign Legionnaires strode about in shiny boots and baggy pants, the orchestra was there for the first time, and Benjy drifted round aimlessly.

There wasn't much to do now except move sets and they'd practised that so often that even he could do it in his sleep. He eyed the chorus enviously, wishing he had a part, even in the back row.

He looked round for Angie, as one of the cardboard scenes wobbled, ominously. Usually, she was on the spot at once, and without her the place seemed strangely empty. Things didn't go smoothly backstage without her.

Benjy frowned, staring at the chorus striding over the desert. Funny. Everyone seemed to miss Angie, and no-one knew why she wasn't there.

He had a sudden horrible thought. Had she left because of him? He'd been rotten to her, but only because he'd been so miserable about Jackie. He mooned around all evening, and wondered why he was so bad tempered.

Then it hit him. He *missed* Angie. Not just her efficiency and orders but everything that was Angie. He sat mournfully on his box as the music swept over him. All he could think of was Angie's stricken eyes, the way her soft curved mouth had trembled at his words.

He didn't even know where she lived, so he couldn't go and apologise. Soon it was time for the last scene change, and the stage manager was shouting at him and the others. They made a mess of it, taking ages to change sets and leaving half the props off the stage.

"What's the matter with you all?" he bellowed.

Benjy picked up a missing chair and hurtled on stage with it, knocking into a cut-out and flattening it. There was an agonised shout, and an elbow stuck out through the hardboard.

Red with embarrassment, he hauled off the palm tree, and there was Angie, hand done up in bandages, lying flat on her back and glowering at him. The chorus was dismissed for a short break while they cleared up the mess.

"Angie! I'm sorry!" Benjy bent to help her up and she pushed him away.

"Look what you've done!" She struggled up, clutching the bent palm tree and gazing in horror at the large hole. "You'll have to do it again! You've ruined it! You idiot!"

"I'm not —" he stammered helplessly. "If you'd been here we wouldn't have left half the props off the stage, and I wouldn't be rushing round like a maniac getting them!"

"So it's *my* fault!" she blazed at him. "I bet you were mooning over Jackie again!"

"I was not!"

Stung, he ignored the stage manager, who was waving his arms furiously at them.

"I was trying to do two jobs, yours and mine! Only, I'm not so

141

good as you, and I can't even cope with mine!"

Despite his outburst, Benjy saw with surprise that she wasn't wearing her glasses. *That* was why she looked so different. Her hair was loose, too, swinging on her shoulders, straight and shiny.

She stood beside him, and suddenly he grabbed her hand.

"Come on. We're in the way."

For once he felt master of the situation. He'd never told Angie what to do before and he thought, jubilantly, maybe he should have tried it. She followed him meekly as he hurried her over to their boxes and pushed her on to hers.

"Where've you been?" he blurted out. "And what have you done to your hand? We've missed you."

"Only because you got in a mess," she said bitterly, and he sat down beside her, feeling oddly shy with her.

"No, Angie," he said soberly. "I missed you because you weren't here. Honest."

"I fell off my bike," she said abruptly. "Had to have my hand bandaged and a tetanus jab, I broke my glasses and haven't got a spare pair, so I'll probably get in an even worse mess than you did. I'll be absolutely useless."

He grinned slowly. "Not if I help you. You tell me what to do, the same as you always do."

She glanced curiously at him, and flushed slowly. "Benjy, I'm sorry, I didn't mean to order you about, but you were so superior you got my back up. It was the only way I could talk to you."

Greatly daring, he put out a hand and pushed a loose tendril of glossy hair back into place.

"Come and have a coffee with me afterwards? At the Sugar Plum?" he asked.

Her face tightened. "What about Jackie? Anyway, you've got that palm tree to fix before you go off."

"Not if you help," he said swiftly. "Anyway, Jackie's not interested in me. And I'm not in her any more."

She watched the chorus straggling off-stage, giggling and laughing, and her face was wistful.

"I would like to have been on stage just once," she said, and he began laughing.

"You were! Under a palm tree!" Suddenly they were laughing together despite the stage manager frantically shushing them.

"Here!" Benjy gasped. "I've got the hammer. You come and hand me the nails and things and we'll do the palm tree together. OK?"

She sat on her box and looked up at him, as the music gathered in volume. Then she got up and stood beside him, holding the palm tree.

"What do we do first?" she asked.

He smiled at her, knowing that this time it *was* different. It really was.

——————— * **THE END** * ———————

JUST A WORD AWAY

> They both had so much to lose. They couldn't see that together they had so much to gain . . .

Complete Story By Patricia Johnstone

WILLIAM brought the file into her office in the middle of Friday afternoon. He looked serious, busy and a shade worn.

He always looked worn and nearly always serious.

"Hello, Emily," he said, just because he had got in from Paris and hadn't seen her since Wednesday.

"Hello." Emily Rogers sat up straight. She was wearing a new blue shift dress and her blonde hair, pageboy style, was shining. She had been expecting to see him today.

She looked up, serious and alert and correct.

"This is it," he said and put the file on her desk. "The new account. I've got a few ideas but I'd like you to look through it first and see what you think."

"Yes, I will." She glanced at him.

"Thanks.

"Did you have a good trip?" she said.

"Not too bad. The flight back was rough."

This was fairly verbose for him.

He stood there in silence and that was exactly the sort of thing that was driving her crazy. *Why* did he stand there and wait?

He put his hand out and touched the file. "This is all we've got. There are no copies and all the sheets are loose inside. I haven't had time to put them in properly."

He would have a reason for standing there, Emily thought. That was the trouble. It always turned out that he had some ordinary casual reason.

"Don't worry. I'll do it."

He nodded his thanks and walked out.

143

Emily got up and looked in the mirror behind her office door. She couldn't see anything wrong with her face. In fact, some people thought it was pretty. It was squarish, grey-eyed, somewhat sun-tanned. Maybe not stunningly lovely, but Emily could see nothing to explain why she and William couldn't talk to each other like two quite ordinary human beings.

She went to the windows and opened one. From the ninth floor of the office block she could see the long street of other offices, some of them taller, some old and low, some where builders were working.

She stood there, her gaze shifting to the pots of African violets on the window-sill, and thought that it couldn't be her fault she and William don't talk to each other.

She had said it all so often to herself.

She had said, *Listen, I love you.*

She had reached out her hand, touched the back of his neck and said, *I always wanted to do that.*

She had said, *Do you remember the day I was going home by bus and you stopped to give me a lift? And then, Mrs Wiley came, too. You won't believe this because it's so silly, but I nearly cried. It was like the end of the world when Mrs Wiley got into your car.*

Do you remember the night when the phone rang in your flat? And when you answered nobody spoke? You sounded so puzzled, so worried. You kept saying "Hello?" in a patient way as though you just had to find out.

I had a reason for phoning. It was quite a good reason, about a book I needed, and then I panicked and just held my breath.

She said all these things when she was falling asleep at night, brushing her teeth in the morning, on the bus going to work, sitting at the launderette hypnotised by the swirl of her clothes in the machine.

She said them a hundred times over and never breathed them to a living soul except herself.

She was 24, old enough to know better — a girl of some ability, and surely intelligent enough to know better.

Yet it didn't help. There was nothing that helped.

She had never, in real life, touched the back of his neck.

HIS name was William Castle. He was older than her — about six years older. He had a streak of grey in his fair hair and it was a little untidy, like his suits and his ties.

He looked like a man with a past. His eyes were greenish and careful. He could have been handsome but it was as though it pleased him better *not* to be handsome. He'd been through it all — the disaster, the pain and the loneliness. He had finished with that, and yet it was there. You could still read the hurt in his eyes.

He was outstandingly good at his work — they all said that. He was a project leader in advertising and there were three others besides Emily on his team. Emily, the newest arrival, had been there four months.

144

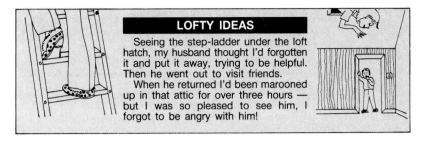

He had enough ideas for them. He flew to Paris and Rome and by the time he came back he knew what he wanted.

They called him William. Everyone was called by their first names here, except Mrs Wiley. Mrs Wiley, however, was in a class of her own, powerful on the secretarial side and obstructive.

They had been calling Emily "Em" since her first week here. They called him William, but not Bill or Will.

She had tried to get more information about him. He'd been married once. But it was over. No-one knew why, but they knew what she meant when she asked. Emily thought this was because once most of them had asked about him, too.

You couldn't ask about William in a casual way.

You had to stop everything dead and say, "But what is he like? When you *really* get to know him, I mean?"

Nobody knew. He was never that close to anyone.

Emily first asked when she'd been there only a few weeks and since then she hadn't tried finding out any more. She didn't know how to try. She'd run out of ideas.

There was only this conversation that went on in her mind.

She said, *There was a day once . . . oh, it was weeks ago. I was standing in the office drinking my coffee. You'd finished yours. Someone had left the morning paper on the desk next to me. You walked past, then you came back and looked at the paper. You bent over it, and your head was so close . . . and I wanted to reach out my hand to touch your hair.*

Emily knew she could never have said that to him.

But there were times when he smiled. She remembered each time. His smiles were sudden and rare with the unintentional charm of a child's.

Which one of us started this? she said. *Oh, I know it was me, but are you sure that it wasn't you, too? How did you get into my thoughts like this? It couldn't have happened from nothing.*

IT was odd that Emily didn't remember the moment of meeting him.

On her first day at work she had been taken round and introduced to everyone in the firm. There were 35 new faces to know, hands to shake, names to learn.

She must have shaken his hand, heard his name, but no bells had rung. There'd been nothing to warn her. Nothing said, "Possibly, this is the man for me."

Anyway, she wondered, when did it start? Was it last month, or earlier?

She didn't know. It had simply happened one day and she knew about it. And once she realised that, she knew that her feeling for William had been going on for some time without her knowing about it.

Yet, there was nothing tangible, nothing she could hold on to.

There was only a moment when she looked up from her desk while he was walking past and their eyes happened to meet.

There was the way he moved closer to her at times — always for good reasons — always with something to do with work.

There was nothing to go building dreams on.

She went out on dates with other men yet they only proved what she already knew. None of them gave her that churned-up, joyful feeling that just thinking about William could bring.

THIS Friday afternoon Emily stood looking down at the city and thought about the weekend when, entirely through choice, she wasn't going out on any dates.

And *he* wasn't either, she felt pretty sure. And in his case it was by choice, too, only he had made the choice long ago and had stuck with it.

And if what she felt for him had been simple friendship she could have done something about it. She could have invited him round for a meal, or suggested a show.

But because she was in love with him she was helpless.

She had to wait for some sign before she could tell him — something better than just a smile.

And when it came she would say, *Listen. I love you.* And she would say it out loud.

★   ★   ★   ★

She had been standing at the window for some time and was amazed to see how much time she had wasted.

She sat down at her desk and went back to her work. It was the artwork for a bicycle advertisement and Emily gave it her full attention. She knew when it was five o'clock.

Footsteps and voices sounded in the passage but she carried on working, feeling guilty about the time she had wasted.

Half an hour later, when everyone had gone, Emily was finished. There was still William's file to look at but that could wait until Monday.

She got up, gathered up her things, then noticed that there was still a window to close . . .

And it was only after she'd closed it that she noticed the bee.

It had been settled on an African violet bloom and now it was buzzing against the glass.

146

"Go on home now," she said, and opened the window. "Let's not all have a gloomy weekend — not all three of us."

The bee moved away from the pane and buzzed against the next window that was still closed.

"All right," she said loudly. "If you can't find the open window I'll have to show you."

Emily reached for a file from her desk, held it steady until the bee crawled on to it and then gently tapped it on the outer window-sill.

The bee flew away to freedom — and the contents of the file slid out, dived downward like ticker-tape into the busy street below.

Emily stared in stark disbelief at the file. Then put it on her desk and opened it.

It was empty and it was William's new account. The one he'd brought back from Paris and had been so pleased about — the one where he had only one copy of all the information.

Emily raced out of the office and along the passage to the lifts. When she reached the ground floor, she tore out of the building and along the pavement more or less below her window.

But it was hopeless.

All she found were two isolated sheets, and during a break in the traffic, she found another.

Half an hour later she walked back to the office wearily.

There was no-one around. Even the cleaners had gone. Soon it would be all locked up. She walked into her office.

GETTING AHEAD

Many readers will think the sight of an elderly gent standing on his bald head on a piece of matting in the middle of the back yard, quite ridiculous.

But my young grandson thought differently.

It all started when I was watching his unsuccessful attempts at headstands. Eventually he gave up and said, "You do it, Grandad."

Fortunately I had done this sort of thing in my youth — and hey-presto, Grandad at the age of 75 did it again.

You've no idea how much I've risen in my grandson's estimation.

WILLIAM was standing by her desk.
"I thought you must have gone home," he said, "and then I saw you hadn't."

Her handbag and shopping parcel were still there.

He stood there and waited while Emily clutched three soiled and crumpled sheets of paper.

"I don't suppose you've had time to look at that new account yet?" he asked.

"Oh, boy." She let out a deep breath and put the three crumpled papers on her desk.

There was a man's heel-print on one.

"That's all there is left of the file," she said. "You see, there happened to be a bee in my office . . ."

To Emily's amazement and astonishment, he laughed — a nice laugh, rich with amusement.

"Don't worry," he said.

"Don't *worry*? But the account?"

"I'll think of something. I'll tell them we've had a fire or that I lost my briefcase. The truth is much better, but you can't expect them to believe . . ." And then he laughed again.

He took a step towards her, put his arms around her and kissed her.

IT was a clumsy kiss. For one thing, Emily was startled. After all the weeks of imagining a scene like this, now that it was happening she felt the same kind of disbelief as when she saw the papers drifting down to the street, and for another thing, he was full of uncertainty.

He had, not without cost, overcome his shyness which she now understood was severe, and he didn't know *how* she felt.

Emily took one step backwards and stared at him.

"Listen . . ." she said.

His eyes made the unambiguous sign she'd waited so long for and she had it all planned what to say next.

"Listen," she said. "I don't know you."

Emily could see clearly that the right things to do and say lay along a very narrow line. All else was blunder.

She could see she had better hold on to the exact truth.

"And you don't know me." She was talking quickly. "And we have to do it right because if we start off like this we're going to have too much to lose, we won't get to know each other."

He listened intently while she went on, "If you ask me if I'm fond of music because you're crazy about it, maybe I won't have the courage and the honesty to say that I never much went for music.

"And so I'll lie to you a little. And maybe you'll lie to me a little. Or maybe we'll pretend that it doesn't matter. And in the end we might have nothing.

"That's why we can't start with a kiss," she said. "We have to know each other. We have to build it up slowly."

They stared at each other in silence.

And then he smiled, his rare smile of unusual charm.

"I can do a lot of slow building," he said, "when I've got a girl who cares what happens to a bee."

Then he took her in his arms and kissed her. And Emily knew it was entirely natural and necessary.

——————— * **THE END** * ———————

The young couple thought they were simply calling a taxi. Little did they know that their call would be answered by —

Cupid On Four Wheels!

Y OU'RE going to the dogs, that's where you're going, Albert Moysey!"

Bert Moysey, with three golden chips impaled on his fork, paused to survey his landlady over the top of his spectacles.

"Matter of fact, I am, Mrs Lomax," he said cheekily. "First race is at six-thirty this —"

"You know full well what I mean!" Audrey Lomax said good-naturedly.

"You could do far more with yourself," Audrey Lomax went on. "I was looking at that dark suit in your wardrobe only yesterday. You haven't worn that since I don't know when. Anyway, I pressed it and polished your black shoes. Just in case of an emergency!"

Bert smiled and turned back to his meal.

"Mmm. No-one makes chips the way you do, Mrs Lomax. Now," he said, looking at his watch, "I'd better be off. Hope it's better than this morning. All local runs they were. I wouldn't mind a long run once in a while. Did I ever tell you . . . ?"

"Yes. Several times," Audrey said and sighed heavily.

"Sorry, Mrs Lomax."

**Complete Story By
MALCOLM WILLIAMS**

"All you ever think about is that taxi of yours!" she added, disappointed her lodger hadn't noticed the new frilly blouse. A little too glamorous for a woman of her age, perhaps, but it *was* her birthday. But *he* didn't know that, and she certainly wasn't going to tell him.

After a few sips he got up and reached for his peaked cap.

"Well now, I'll be off," he said. "Mustn't keep old Betsy waiting."

"The way you talk about that taxi you'd think it was a woman!"

"Well, Betsy and me have been together now for eighteen years, Mrs L."

"I know — *and it don't seem a day too much!*" She sighed, helping him into his raincoat. "If ever a man was married to his taxi, it's you, Albert Moysey!"

"Ta for the lunch then."

149

"Will you want tea? Or will you be going straight to the dogs?"
Her irony was lost on him.

"I'll be back later tonight," he said. "See you then."

She watched him drive off down the tree-lined street then dropped the lounge curtain. Nearly a year Bert had been lodging with her now. He was very comfortable here — and spoiled, Audrey reflected. Yet, she liked mothering him.

Since his wife had died 10 years ago he must have had a lonely life. As a widow, she knew that.

Opening the few envelopes she'd received that morning, she displayed her birthday cards on the mantelpiece. She hadn't brought them out before. She hadn't wanted Bert to think she was hinting.

But all the same it would have been nice if he'd made some kind of gesture just for once. Still, she reasoned, how was he to know it was her birthday?

B ERT cruised around Piccadilly Circus on the chance of picking up a random fare.

As he came round for a second time, a young man held out a newspaper. Betsy pulled smoothly to a halt. Bert rolled down his window.

"Where to then, guv?" he asked in his throaty voice.

The young man glanced at the attractive girl beside him but she looked up at the sky. He showed Bert a flight schedule.

"Can you get me to Heathrow in time for this flight?"

Bert grinned. "It's quite a distance to the airport, guv, but I've never failed yet!"

Setting his meter, he glanced into the driving mirror. The girl stood uncertainly on the pavement clutching her bag. The young man on the back seat leaned forward to look up at her.

"Are you coming or aren't you, Chris?"

The girl compressed her lips, shrugged, then reluctantly got into the taxi beside him.

"Mind closing your door, dear?" Bert asked.

The man reached over and closed the door and Bert saw the girl tense up against him.

Then there was a big gap between them on the seat as they both sat back. The young man caught Bert's eye in the mirror.

Bert smiled. "Nice day, isn't it, guv? Great to see the sun."

"Terrific!" he replied with studied irony.

Bert rested his elbow out of the driving window. "Here we go, Betsy. Back into the chariot race."

He put the taxi into gear and, leaving the passenger's connecting window open, moved into the stream of traffic . . .

I N the back, the girl sat stiffly, looking out of her window as Bert guided Betsy in and out of the traffic.

"Cigarette, Chris?"

"Thank you, Roy."

She took one from his cigarette case and waited for him to click his lighter. Then she stared out at the traffic again.

"What's up, Chris, cat got your tongue?" Roy asked.

"I can't think of anything to say," she told him curtly. "Anyway, you seem to be the exclusive topic of conversation these days."

"Ouch!" Roy said. "All right, let's talk about you, then."

She shrugged. "Well, you know me — good old faithful Chris. Always around . . ."

"Come on, Chris, don't be like that." He pushed back a stray wave of hair from his forehead.

They both glanced at the yawning space between them, then turned away.

"I suppose once you've put me on the plane to Manchester, that'll be me out of your way," she said.

Roy looked at her, obviously puzzled.

Bert could see the unhappiness on her face.

"Are you wishing you hadn't come down to London?" he said tiredly. "I thought you'd be pleased about the new job."

Just then he turned and saw Bert watching him in the mirror. Both men pretended they hadn't noticed each other and Roy looked out at the busy streets.

After a long, heavy silence, Roy tried again.

"Look, Chris, I don't understand you when you're like this. You seemed so pleased when I passed the interview last month. I told you then I couldn't have got through it without you . . ."

"As I said, good old faithful Chris," she said without turning.

"Look, Chris." This time she did look, straight into his eyes, "I . . . I'm sorry I flew at you after the meeting. My enthusiasm carried me away.

"The final details of my posting date, the prospect of working abroad, the excitement of everything. I thought you'd have shared my enthusiasm."

"It's all right," she said stiffly. "Don't worry about it."

Suddenly the girl's eyes met Bert's in the mirror. He stared straight ahead, intent on the traffic. Soon they would be approaching Heathrow Airport.

"There was no need to come by taxi, Roy. It's too expensive."

"It's all right, Chris. Anyway, we can't have you hanging about for airport buses."

"I think I should have gone back by train this time," she said.

"Nonsense — nothing's too good for you. I wanted you here as long as possible."

"I'm very pleased for you, Roy," she said. "Really I am. I don't think I even remembered to congratulate you. After all, you didn't *really* believe it was all happening until today, did you? I mean, even after the interview you thought something would go wrong."

"I suppose you're right, Chris. You know me, the eternal pessimist."

"Huh! Well, I don't know why. We plodders are the ones who should be pessimists."

"Don't say that, Chris. You're not a plodder — anything but. Remember, we spent most of our school days together. Even the same university."

She looked absently out of his window this time. "Yes, Roy. Almost a lifetime's habit, aren't I?"

She gave him no chance to comment.

"I'll give your regards to everyone, Roy. And my parents will be eager to know all about it. Will you write to me from South America?"

"Of course!"

"As long as it's not in Spanish then. Languages aren't my scene, as you know."

"Chris. Stop knocking yourself."

"I'm not knocking myself. I'm the eternal realist. Remember?"

"Oh, for goodness' sake, Chris —"

"Goodness nothing! I'm just sitting here telling myself how lucky I am. A good steady job which is killing me with boredom. Friends who are killing me with sympathy. And Mum and Dad — they're killing me with kindness.

"After all," her voice rose harshly, "it's not every day a girl can boast of a boyfriend who's going to spend the rest of his life in Cairo and Caracas and . . . and Casablanca. I mean, if *I'm* lucky, my department may post me to Cardiff!"

"It's not like that, Chris," he said angrily. "I won't go to any of those places. After all —"

"You told me so yourself. After this morning you told me you'd be spending about two-thirds of your career overseas. You'll come back to London for refresher courses, to recharge your batteries, then you'll be off to Timbuktu at the drop of a hat!

"Oh, yes, you told me. Diplomatically, of course, but then you're the budding diplomat, Roy, the up and coming —" She broke off as a great roar sounded overhead.

A giant jet airliner was making its landing approach, flaps and undercarriage down. It entirely deafened whatever he said next.

THE plane's roar receded. Fractionally composed, Christine fumbled for a handkerchief and blew her nose.

"All right, Chris," he grunted. "I asked for it. I was the one to suggest that we talk about you. But I didn't expect an outburst like that."

"*What?*" She stared truculently at him. "Would you mind explaining, Roy?"

"Look, Chris —"

"You're always saying that! I *am* looking. And waiting. The trouble with me is I've always let you take me for . . . for granted!"

"Keep your voice down!" They both stared at Bert but he was staring straight ahead.

"I've always propped you up, Roy Noble. At school, at university — even now when you've left home and should be standing on your own two feet."

"Christine, I've never taken you for granted," he said softly. "I've relied on you. Of course I have. But we grew up together. And most of all . . ."

"Yes, Roy? Most of all?"

"Most of all, Chris, I've always depended on your love. What I mean is, Chris —"

"You're giving me the brush-off. Well, it's my own stupid fault. You've worked me out of your system, and I've helped you do it."

"No, Chris!"

Ahead, Bert could see an airport sign, standing out like a giant neon light. Two miles. Only a few minutes . . .

Christine was fighting back the tears now.

"I've tried to stand on my own feet, Chris. But —"

"There's no need to explain, Roy."

"But I must!"

"I should have kept out of your way, for the past two years. Then you'd have found your own salvation."

"But that's what I'm trying to explain to you —"

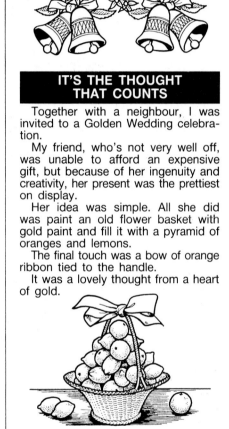

IT'S THE THOUGHT THAT COUNTS

Together with a neighbour, I was invited to a Golden Wedding celebration.

My friend, who's not very well off, was unable to afford an expensive gift, but because of her ingenuity and creativity, her present was the prettiest on display.

Her idea was simple. All she did was paint an old flower basket with gold paint and fill it with a pyramid of oranges and lemons.

The final touch was a bow of orange ribbon tied to the handle.

It was a lovely thought from a heart of gold.

Suddenly Betsy's engine died. Roy and Christine looked up in surprise. They were in a line of traffic. Thirty yards ahead the traffic lights were changing to green. The cars in front began to move forward. Betsy didn't budge.

"What's wrong, cabby?" Roy asked in concern.

Bert turned. "Don't worry, guv. I'll have you away in a jiff."

Christine glanced anxiously behind. Cars were pulling out and overtaking them, most of them impatiently tooting their horns.

Continued on page 157

OH, FOR SOME PARTY PEACE

By
RONI
BORDEN

IF prospective parents knew the true facts about the planning and execution of a child's birthday party, population growth would probably grind to a halt! Moreover, the facts cannot be learned from the toy and sweets manufacturers, who never see beyond the end of the cash register, but from a mother who has been through it all and survived. A mother like me.

The trouble starts a month or so before the event with threats like:

"If you don't let me ride your new bicycle I won't let you come to my birthday party."

"If I can't have a lick of your lollipop you can't come to my party."

These are actually idle threats though, as any child will invite everyone in sight who is willing to bring a present. In fact, if the child were old enough to copy names and addresses from the telephone book, the list would probably increase even more!

The next problem is to decide where to have the party. Bowling alleys are places where things are really meant to be knocked down and so would seem like the ideal place for the rough and tumble of a birthday party. But since the alleys wisely allow only a few children at a time, the setting isn't acceptable to the birthday child who doesn't want his numbers —

Once a year, whether you like it or not, your child has a birthday. And if you can't ignore his pleas for a party, Roni Borden has some hints on how to survive it — more or less intact!

and presents — limited.

The local fish and chip shop is a good place, too. If there is a sound-proofed room in the back, so that it won't spoil the appetites of the rest of the clientèle. But the price can be prohibitive — eating out for thirty-five children can be expensive.

So the only thing left is to roll up your rugs, put the furniture in storage and prepare for the attack.

The menu for the party should be all the favourite foods of the birthday child. This always turns out to be all the things that give children bad teeth and make them ill. But don't worry about this, since the food won't end up in anyone's mouth anyway!

The only food that children

actually eat at a birthday party is food that has been thrown across the room and accidentally lands in someone's mouth.

The next things to plan are the games.

If the birthday child is under six, all the games have to be devised so that he can win. Otherwise he might disappear under his bed, taking all his presents with him.

To avoid this, prepare him a special blindfold with a hole in it for him when he plays Pin The Tail On The Donkey and strategically disqualify a few kids during the relay races.

If the child is over six, however, the games have to be devised so that all the children win. The only way to get round this is to have a first prize, a second prize, a third prize . . . a thirty-fourth prize, for every game — and everyone will go home happy.

The types of games that you select are important.

Musical Chairs is good because the longer you continue to play the music and the longer the children have to walk (that means run or push) around the chairs, the less time you have left to do anything else.

Relay races are good for using up energy, but no matter how many children you invite, or how carefully you check on it, you always end up with an odd number of children.

This leaves an unequal number of children competing, unless, of course, you join one team, handicapping yourself by running on your knees.

THE high point of the afternoon is opening up the presents. Then all the children make a circle around the birthday child, and he proceeds to open the cards and gifts.

By this time at least six wrappings have come loose, so it's a little hard to tell who brought what. Quietly, the birthday child has to say:

"I want to thank whoever brought this gift."

No doubt there will be some response, like:

"I brought that game because my mother couldn't find anything cheaper in the store," or "I brought that gift because my uncle brought me one when he came to visit but I already had it."

Once the presents are open, the party sort of disintegrates, because all the children make a mad lunge for all the new toys, ignoring the rest of the world.

When the time finally arrives to send everyone home, there is chocolate cake on the floor and walls, ice-cream and sausage rolls on the chairs and a massive pile of broken toys in the middle of the room. Don't worry — these are sure signs of a successful party.

The final job of the birthday child is to write "Thank you" notes to all his little friends. Mother has to be very careful to check these out, however, to be sure he doesn't send such winners as:

"Dear Jimmy, I would have liked this gift a lot better if I hadn't already got one from my aunt," or "Dear Julie, I didn't like what you got me and next year you can't come to my birthday party."

I have often thought of giving my children up for adoption on the day before their birthdays and taking them back the day after, but as no-one will take me up on this, I console myself with the fact that birthdays come only once a year. ∎

COW, BOY!

Early one morning — I couldn't believe my eyes! There in our back garden, calmly munching our rose bushes, was a big brown cow from the field next door.

She wasn't worried, but I was. I just had to get her back where she belonged, before she completely ruined my husband's beautifully-tended garden.

Pushing, shouting and whistling at her had no effect. Nor did a hose of cold water, or even a tempting box full of sugar lumps.

I was just about at my wits' end when my neighbour's miniature poodle saved the day. In true sheepdog fashion, he came bounding through the hedge and began to circle the cow, barking. The poor, frightened animal then immediately took off for her own field.

You could have knocked me down with a feather — I'd no idea the little dog had been getting secret lessons from Lassie!

Continued from page 153

Bert kept turning the ignition key, but Betsy only grunted.

He released the bonnet catch, opened his door and got out.

"Good job I didn't get stuck right up at the lights." He grinned to the couple in the back. Then he lifted the bonnet lid and disappeared beneath it.

"GO and see if you can help, Roy!" Bert heard the girl say in a rather worried voice.

"*Me?*"

"You're the man!"

Roy uncomfortably shifted his weight on the seat.

Christine glanced at him. "Well, shall *I* get out and help?"

Reluctantly, Roy got out and walked to the front. Bert was leaning right over the engine, peering intently.

"What seems to be the trouble then?" Roy asked.

"Trouble?" Bert studied him over the top of his spectacles.

"Were you having a spot of trouble then, guv?" He winked. "With the young lady, I mean."

Roy flushed. "You heard what was going on?"

"Couldn't help overhearing, guv," Bert said.

Roy stared at the engine. "Can you fix this?"

"If you really want me to."

"Huh?"

Roy stared uncomprehendingly into Bert's face. Bert winked over his specs.

"Er," Roy whispered, "did you make the car stop on purpose?"

Bert gave him an enigmatic grin.

"The thing about Betsy is . . ." He patted the radiator cap. "The thing about this taxi is she's just like a woman."

He smiled benignly now, but Roy looked mystified.

"Woman?"

"Yes. She does what I tell her to do. She respects me 'cos I'm firm. But I've got to be fair, too, y'see. I've got to tell her what I expect of her . . ."

Roy's eyes glazed over. "But I don't know anything about car engines," he said, waving helplessly at the leads and hoses.

"Ah! But when it comes to women, guv?"

Roy straightened up, pushing his hand through his hair. Bert noticed Christine winding down the passenger window.

"Roy! What on earth's happening? Do you know what the time is!"

Roy looked at his watch and gasped. He joined Bert behind the bonnet again.

Oblivious to the constant stream of aircraft landing and taking off above them, Roy and Bert had their heads close together. Bert, in layman's terms, was explaining:

"And so you see, guv, all I did was pull the choke out. And she flooded, poor old thing. The more I turned the engine, the more she protested!"

A bright smile spread across Roy's face. "Fantastic! But can you start her again?"

"Start?" Bert said indignantly. "Betsy'll do anything I tell her to." With a grin he added, "But I've got to *tell her*, y'see."

By the time Roy got back into the taxi, Bert had pushed in the choke. At the second turn of the engine, Betsy growled obediently. They slipped back into the stream of traffic.

He glanced at his watch. If he didn't exactly put his foot down, they should arrive *just* in time to see the Manchester flight take off.

"WHY is he going so slow?" Christine hissed.

"Traffic conditions," Roy said worriedly.

"Why are you looking so glum?" Christine asked.

"Sorry, Chris. I was just hoping . . ."

"Hoping what?"

He licked a dry lip. "What I was trying to say to you before we broke down . . ."

Suddenly, she started grinning at him.

"There's no need to ridicule me, Chris. I know I'm not very good

158

It's Your Move . . .

"OH, I wouldn't like to . . ."

These words were spoken by a friend of mine the other day and they brought me to the firm conclusion that one of our most deeply ingrained characteristics is shyness.

We were both sitting looking at a huge batch of cakes and scones she'd made for a party that had been called off at the last minute.

"What in the world am I to do with all this?" she wailed.

"Mrs Next-door," I suggested, remembering the team of youngsters always whooping round the next-door garden.

That was when my friend said, "Oh, I wouldn't like to offer them . . . She might think it a bit pushing of me."

In the end she did make her offering. It was accepted with gratitude — and demolished with whoops of delight by those back-garden Cowboys and Indians.

But it made me wonder just how many times we decide not to make the small friendly gesture, the unexpected gift, the offer of help or friendliness because we "don't want to seem pushing."

Oh, I know there are a few unresponsive, fiercely independent people in the world. But how very few they must be compared with all those who are only too willing and eager to be friendly.

Maybe they're waiting for us to make the first move. It would be a pity if self-consciousness and shyness kept us from making it, wouldn't it?

at expressing my feelings but —"

She giggled, in spite of the situation.

"What's wrong?" he demanded.

"You! You've got a smudge of oil right on the end of your nose."

He rubbed his nose. That only made it worse and Christine burst out laughing.

Bert winked at him in the driving mirror.

"I don't think we're going to make it, guv!" he announced.

"Not going to make it!" Christine echoed, taking her vanity mirror from her bag. She looked shrewdly at Roy, lowering her voice.

"He sounds very cheerful about it! He promised to get us there in . . .

"Roy Noble, you're looking smug."

"Me? Smug? Never!" Roy studied his nose in her vanity mirror.

She passed him a tissue and he wiped off most of the oil.

"What are you up to, Roy?"

"Nothing. I haven't done a thing. It wasn't *me* that broke down, was it?"

"No but . . ."

They turned into the long tunnel leading into the airport terminals.

"It's all right, Chris," Roy said, looking at his watch. "You'll never catch that plane now."

"*What?*" She stared at him in bewilderment.

"I don't want you to catch that plane, Chris. I want you to marry me. I can't go abroad without you. Surely you know that . . ."

Then he reached forward and closed the partition glass.

BERT MOYSEY didn't hear what else was said, but in his mirror he noticed that suddenly there wasn't a gap between the couple any more.

Roy drew Christine against him and kissed her. Bert looked away contentedly then he turned round at the terminal without even stopping and headed straight back towards London . . .

An hour or so later he let himself into the house and found the note from his landlady.

Just popped out, will be back soon, Mrs L.

"Couldn't be better," Bert congratulated himself, laying down the enormous bunch of flowers he'd bought on the way home.

It was true, he reflected, he was guilty of taking his landlady for granted. Time he took her out for an evening. He'd placed the flowers in water before he noticed the birthday cards on the mantelpiece.

"By jingo, if it's not her birthday!" he gasped.

★   ★   ★   ★

Audrey Lomax was amazed to see the taxi standing outside the house when she returned with some shopping. She looked at her wristwatch and shook it in disbelief. Her lodger should have been at the greyhound stadium now.

"Albert! You home — ?"

She stopped short in the kitchen doorway — not only at the sight of the beautiful flowers standing in her best china jug, but at Albert, waiting there in white shirt, his dark suit and black shiny shoes.

"Albert Moysey!" Her fingers fluttered to her lips. "I can't believe it!"

"Happy birthday, Mrs L. Just a little surprise."

"Oh, Albert!"

Audrey buried her face in the flowers to conceal her tears of delight. For the first time ever he took her heavy shopping bag from her.

"Hope you haven't been buying us any supper, Mrs L. I'm taking you out on the town tonight. Somewhere smart, mind. In that classy blouse, I could take you anywhere!"

"Oh, Albert!" Audrey exclaimed, shiny-eyed. "And all the time you knew it was my birthday!"

"Well, er," Bert coughed modestly, "you didn't really think I was going to the dogs, did you? Not on your birthday!"

——————— * **THE END** * ———————

Cry Baby

He sulked,
he threw tantrums
about nothing —
and that was
just her husband!

Complete Story
By EMMA CLARE

I KNEW he would!" Tracy announced.

"Knew he'd what?" her mother asked.

"Walk right past Mark's pram without looking at him — he always does. Don't you?" She almost threw the words at the bewildered culprit as he stepped inside the door.

"Don't I what?" Eric Dawson asked, dumping his briefcase with relief.

"Ignore your son! You didn't look in the pram again."

"Oh, Tracy, be reasonable! He isn't likely to have changed drastically since this morning."

"You didn't look at him then, either," she accused.

"I didn't need to. Since there weren't any ear-splitting vibrations shattering the peace, I knew he wasn't in his pram!" he retaliated.

"Well, I must be off soon," Tracy's mother broke in a little too brightly. "Your father will be in before I am and he hates arriving home to an empty house."

"He doesn't know when he's well off," Eric muttered, scowling at the pram, from which gurgling sounds were already escaping.

"Well, I'm going to freshen up with a shower before supper." And he wrenched his tie off.

"Please do. I'm sure I'll manage to fry the chops, make the bottle and quieten Mark on my own."

The door slammed and Tracy found herself talking to the two coats hanging there. Pushing her dishevelled hair behind her ears, she knew she looked an absolute mess.

She was still wearing the crumpled jeans and top she'd pulled on, in a semi-conscious state, at quarter-to-six that morning.

Now they were sadly the worse for wear with their various milk and rusk stains and streaks of baby powder.

Where, she wondered miserably, was the girl of a year ago, with her high ideals of radiant motherhood? Somewhere among the dozens of nappies, endless feeds and disturbed nights she had got lost.

Her mother didn't help matters, either. She stood there gathering up her things, looking so fresh with her slim figure and smart up-to-date suit. She only made Tracy feel even more drab and doubly aware of the unwanted inches around her middle.

"I don't think Eric loves the baby much at all, Mum," she told her tearfully.

"Of course he does. He just doesn't know him yet. All the baby seems to have done so far is monopolise his wife and give him very little in return.

"Perhaps if you tried remembering that Eric is your husband as well as your son's father, and showed him that he is still important to you, it might help."

"Mother, Mark is six weeks old. Have you tried coping with a demanding baby and proving to a temperamental husband that he's all-important at the same time?" Tracy protested hotly.

"Yes, dear, I have. Several times."

"But Dad's always been a devoted father. I couldn't see him ignoring Mark."

"Perhaps not now," her mother agreed, "but sometimes devoted fathers are *made*, rather than born. Believe me, yours did his fair share of sulking and feeling sorry for himself when you were howling your way through every day and night."

Mrs Thompson put both hands gently on her daughter's drooping shoulders.

"But once he got to know you, and could boast once in a while that he could quieten you when I couldn't, he became as devoted as the rest."

That's as may be, thought Tracy later, balancing a raging Mark on her hip while preparing his bottle, but this particular father stood little chance of getting to know his son at all. When he wasn't buried behind his newspaper, or hiding under his pillow, he fled to the garden every time his son and heir had a good howl.

I STILL say he'd be better in his own room," Eric whispered later, as they groped their way around the dark bedroom getting ready for bed.

"We might not hear him," Tracy objected.

"You must be joking! When he decides to air his lungs, the other end of the street can hear him!"

"Eric, come here and listen!"

"Where's here, for heaven's sake?"

"By the cot." Tracy's voice was muffled as she bent down. "Can you hear him breathing?"

"Give me strength," Eric pleaded despairingly to the ceiling.

"Shh, you'll wake him."

"Shh, you'll wake him," Eric mimicked in a frustrated whisper. "If he's awake it's 'Talk to him, Eric, you never talk to him,' and if he's asleep, it's 'Shh, Eric, you'll wake him.' Ow!"

"Shh. What have you done *now*?"

"There you go again with your shushing. I've stubbed my toe, *again*. Not for the first or the second time but for the *third time* tonight. So please, Tracy, between now and tomorrow, make up your mind. Either he moves into the spare room or I do."

Long after Eric was asleep Tracy lay staring into the darkness. Tomorrow, when she went to see Dr Marshall, she would tell him about Eric's growing antagonism towards the baby. Whatever her mother said, it couldn't be normal.

Why, he was even threatening to throw him out into the spare room. Just what kind of a brute had she married, she wondered. Then she fell asleep.

VISITING Dr Marshall was like visiting an old friend. Tracy had known him all her life and had worked as his receptionist from leaving school until before Mark was born.

His welcome was whole-hearted and warm.

He stood up as she entered, extending a big, capable hand in greeting. "Tracy, it's good to see you again. How are you?"

Everything about Dr Marshall was big, Tracy thought. He was one of the world's big, gentle, compassionate men.

"You're looking tired," he observed. "Is that new son of yours keeping you on your toes too much?"

His sympathetic manner brought a lump to her throat. The next moment she found herself sobbing in a constant stream of tissues about burps that wouldn't burp, spare bedrooms and Eric stubbing his toe every night.

Dr Marshall let her finish dabbing.

"It strikes me that young man just doesn't know what having a baby around the place entails," he said. "Why don't you let him have a go sometimes?

"Let him give Mark his ten o'clock feed occasionally and get yourself off for a long lazy bath and an early night with a good book."

"Read?" Tracy said, a faint smile playing on her lips. "I couldn't read if Eric was seeing to the baby. Why, he won't even hold him if

Continued on page 166

163

TOP *for Versatility*

Materials Required – Of **Patons Pure Wool Crepe Double Knit,** 5 (5, 6, 6) x 50 gram balls main colour; 3 (3, 4, 4) x 50 gram balls contrast; 4.50 mm crochet hook; 5 buttons.

For best results it is essential to use the recommended yarn. If you have difficulty in obtaining the yarn, write direct, enclosing a stamped addressed envelope, to the following address for stockists: Customer Liaison Department, Patons & Baldwins, Kilncraigs, Alloa, Clackmannanshire FK10 1EG. Tel: 0259 723431.

Measurements – To fit 86 (91, 97, 102) centimetre, *34 (36, 38, 40) inch*, bust; actual measurement, 91 (97, 102, 107) centimetres, *36 (38, 40, 42) inches*; length at centre back, 54 centimetres, *21¼ inches*.

Tension – 16 stitches and 12 rows to 10 centimetres, *4 inches*, measured over pattern using 4.50 mm crochet hook.

Abbreviations – **Ch.** – chain; **d.c.** – double crochet; **tr.** – treble; **t.ch.** – turning chain; **st.(s)** – stitch(es); **sl.-st.** – slip stitch; **M** – main colour; **C** – contrast; **cm** – centimetres; **ins** – inches.

N.B. Figures in brackets ( ) refer to the larger sizes; where only one figure is given, this refers to all sizes.

PATTERN (repeat of 2 sts. + 2 for base chain).

1st row (right side) – 2 tr. into 4th ch. from hook, *miss 1 ch., 2 tr. into next ch.; repeat from * to last 2 ch., miss 1 ch., 1 tr. into last ch.

2nd row – 3 ch., *miss 2 sts., 2 tr. between 2nd missed st. and next st.; repeat from * to last 2 sts., miss 1 st., 1 tr. into t.ch.

Repeat 2nd row for pattern using M and C alternately to give stripes.

Whether the occasion is stylish and smart, or comfortable and casual, this crocheted waistcoat will add the finishing touch to your outfit.

BACK

With 4.50 mm hook and M make 62 (66, 70, 74) ch. and work 1st row – 60 (64, 68, 72) sts.

Join in C and work 2nd row. Repeat 2nd row working M and C alternately to give stripes, at the same time increase 1 st. at each end of next and every following alternate row until there are 74 (78, 82, 86) sts. Continue without shaping until work measures 26 cm, *10¼ ins.*

Shape Armholes

Next row – Sl.-st. over first 4 sts., pattern to last 4 sts., turn. Continue in pattern, decreasing 1 st. at each end of next and every following alternate row until 58 (62, 66, 70) sts. remain. Continue without shaping until work measures 50 cm, *19¾ ins.*

Shape Shoulders

Next row – Sl.-st. over first 7 (8, 9, 10) sts., pattern to last 7 (8, 9, 10) sts., turn.

Next row – Sl.-st. over first 8 (9, 10, 11) sts., pattern to last 8 (9, 10, 11) sts., turn – 28 sts. Fasten off.

POCKET LININGS

With 4.50 mm hook and M make 18 ch. and work in d.c. Decrease 1 st. at each end of every alternate row until 2 sts. remain. Work 1 row. Fasten off.

without shaping until work measures 35 cm, *13¾ ins*, from beginning of point.

Front Shaping

Keeping pattern correct decrease 1 st. at front edge on next and every following alternate row until side edge of work measures same as back to armhole shaping, ending at side edge.

Shape Armhole

Keeping front shaping correct as before on every alternate row.

Next row – Sl.-st. over first 4 sts., pattern to end. Decrease 1 st. at armhole edge on every following alternate row 4 times, then keeping armhole edge straight continue with front shaping until 15 (17, 19, 21) sts. remain. Continue without shaping until armhole measures same as on back, ending at armhole edge.

Shape Shoulder

Next row – Sl.-st. over first 7 (8, 9, 10) sts., pattern to end. Fasten off.

RIGHT FRONT

Work as for left front, reversing all shaping and working pocket insertion row in reverse.

EDGINGS AND TO MAKE UP

Join side seams, matching stripes. Join shoulder seams.

With 4.50 mm hook and M work 4 rows of d.c. round front points, back cast-on edge and armholes.

On right front mark positions for 5 buttonholes, the first to come 1 cm, *⅜ inch*, from beginning and the last at beginning of front shaping, with the others spaced evenly between. Work 5 rows in d.c. round front edges and neck, working buttonholes at marked positions on 3rd row as follows: at each marked place work 2 ch., miss 2 d.c. Sew on buttons to match buttonholes.

Sew pocket linings in place. ∎

LEFT FRONT

With 4.50 mm hook and M make 4 ch. and work 1st row. Working in stripes as on back, work 1 row. Increase one st. at front edge and 2 sts. at side edge on every row until there are 32 (34, 36, 38) sts. Pattern 2 rows.

Insert Pocket (Side Edge)

In correct colour, pattern 8 (10, 12, 14) sts., pattern across 16 sts. of pocket lining, miss next 16 sts., pattern 8. Work 2 rows. Increase 1 st. at side edge on next and every following alternate row until there are 36 (38, 40, 42) sts. Continue

Continued from page 163

he can help it, and when he does he looks as though he's going to drop him any minute. If that happened I'd never forgive myself."

Dr Marshall smiled benignly. "Surprising though it may seem, Tracy, I have never yet heard of a father dropping his baby and I've seen some pretty awkward-looking ones in my time, I can tell you. How is he ever going to get used to handling him if he never has any practice, eh?"

"He doesn't want to practise," Tracy persisted. "He doesn't even look at him very often."

"Then it's about time somebody showed him what he's missing," Dr Marshall said before changing the subject. "What time's your bus?"

"A quarter-to-six. Why?"

"Good, then you've time for a cup of tea with me. You're my last patient and Esther is away visiting her sister for the day.

"Come on, we'll go through to the house and you can tell me all your troubles — and I bet you can't think of one I haven't heard a thousand times before."

IT was a considerably happier Tracy who left some time later to catch her bus. Maybe it had been Dr Marshall's sympathetic ear, or the tea, or perhaps it had been sitting in a room that wasn't cluttered with baby clothes, but whatever it was, it had worked.

However, 10 minutes later Tracy was back, wide-eyed and distraught.

"I've missed the bus," she blurted out, "and there isn't another for an hour. Mark will need feeding and . . . his bottle isn't ready . . . and . . . oh, Dr Marshall, Eric won't have a clue what to do."

Dr Marshall took his pocket-watch out with almost deliberate slowness.

"Let me see now," he said. "Oh dear, yes, it's ten past six. I'll have to get that sitting-room clock fixed. It's not at all reliable these days.

"Never mind, no harm done, I'll get the car out and run you home before they've even missed you."

"No harm done!" Tracy paced up and down as Dr Marshall disappeared off to the garage. "A starving baby, an incompetent husband and he says there's no harm done!"

She thought she would scream.

"Right, Tracy, ready when you are," Dr Marshall called at last.

Never had anyone taken so long to do such a short journey, Tracy thought. They cruised up to the third set of traffic lights and they promptly turned red.

"Don't look so worried," Dr Marshall said gently. "That husband of yours will probably be coping a lot better than you imagine. Why, when my eldest was a couple of months old I looked after him single-handed for two whole days and I knew no more about it than Eric does.

"Measles, mumps, yes! Delivering the little blighters, yes! But nappies and bottles. I hadn't a clue!"

"Was your wife ill or something?" Tracy asked, horrified at the thought of Eric taking over for two hours, let alone two days.

"Good heavens, no. Esther's never ill, at least she never admits she is. No," he said, and chuckled. "She walked out on me!"

"Walked out on you?" Tracy's voice was incredulous. "Left you holding the baby?"

"Yes, exactly that. And I asked for it. I only knew what I'd read about rearing babies and I was convinced my wife was the most incompetent woman alive.

"So, I sulked when my meals weren't ready, moaned when the baby cried and hid my head under the pillow when he woke up in the night, until she walked out and left me to get on with it."

"But what did you do?" Tracy asked.

"I coped, after a fashion. And when Esther came back, as I'd known she would all along, I felt I knew a lot more about my own son. And I wasn't quite so quick to criticise again.

"I think he even sympathised with his dad a bit, too, because in the middle of my third catastrophic nappy-changing session, he gave me his first real smile. It was marvellous — it really stretched from ear to ear.

"I don't think Esther has ever quite forgiven me for being cheated out of that!"

THE car drew up to a leisurely halt outside Tracy's house. Tracy's spine prickled at the utter silence everywhere. It was *too* quiet.

If Mark had been yelling or Eric cursing it would have been worrying — but this uncanny silence was unnerving.

Her heart thumped madly as she opened the door of the lounge.

"Eric, I'm sorry I'm late, I . . ."

"Shh. Close the door quietly."

He was sitting in an armchair, the tenderly-wrapped bundle asleep on his shoulder, the smooth, dark head resting against Eric's cheek.

An empty feeding bottle stood on the table and far from seeming awkward, Eric looked as though he was a veteran parent.

"Have you been all right?" she asked.

"Shh," Eric whispered again. "You'll wake him. Of course we've been all right. I've been looking at his ears, though. Do you think the right one sticks out more than the other?"

Tracy shook her head but said nothing.

"Hey, guess what he did?" Eric went on.

"What?" Tracy asked, guessing the answer already.

"He gave me his first real smile."

"One that stretched from ear to ear?" she asked.

"Yes, a real beauty. Why?"

"Oh, nothing," she said, and kissed the top of one dark head and then the other.

———— ∗ **THE END** ∗ ————

THE two old ladies sat in the shelter on the promenade watching the sea. It stretched like silver tinfoil to the distant shimmering horizon.

They'd sat there every day through the long, hot summer, not speaking much, each eating the cake and fruit they'd picked for themselves. They weren't really all that old — Ada Calthorpe was 60 and her sister, Edith, 61.

Each was busy with her own thoughts. Ada's were mostly of how she could get rid of Edith. Not anything as drastic as murder, just a gentle kind of persuasion to encourage her to go away and leave her alone.

It was August — holiday time. Children of all ages swarmed over the beach like brightly-coloured insects — toddlers up-ended as they tried to stagger to the curling waves, older ones digging purposefully at sandcastles, some riding the donkeys, and nearly all licking ice-creams as they shouted at each other, or their parents or "Nannas."

Ada didn't really approve of the way children today called their grandmothers Nanna or Nanny. All her life she'd been called that, at least for nearly 50 years of it. But it had meant what it said then.

TWO'S A CROWD!

• Complete Story By JUDY CHARD •

A nanny was someone who was more often than not an unshifting rock of solidarity in an unstable world, something a small child could cling to until he or she found their own feet. Someone who lived out her life in various nurseries, comforting, bathing, feeding and some-times scolding, other people's babies . . .

And now, at last, she had her very own little house subscribed for by a number of her late employers. Several of them would have liked Nanny to settle permanently within call. They'd said, "It's too late to set up a home of your own now, Nanny."

They'd offered little self-contained flats over stables, the empty gardener's cottage, a gamekeeper's house in the woods . . . Ada had been deeply touched by their thoughtfulness, but she'd refused all offers.

Never in the whole of her 60 years had she owned any place she could have entirely to herself. Always before, her bedroom, living-room, even bathroom had been shared with the current family's babies.

168

Not that she'd minded, but how wonderful it was to have her own home at last. Those years of other people's houses had given her an intense longing for her very own place, where she could shut the front door and be alone.

Her only remaining relative had been deeply shocked at the idea of her wanting to live alone.

Everything in the garden was lovely. Then came a visit from that domineering, interfering old busybody — her sister!

"You've been among children too long, Ada," her sister Edith said. "It's affected your brain."

She sniffed as Ada explained she was very sorry, but she didn't want to share with her elder sister. "Sign you're getting senile, wanting to be alone," she added.

Ada didn't care what anyone thought or said. Edith hadn't bothered with her much in the past anyway. She'd been a widow for 10 years now, and never even invited Ada to spend any holiday she might have with her. So now Ada was determined to look after herself.

When she'd first got the little cottage, a mile or two from a big south coast seaside town, she'd felt like a queen as she looked round the tiny parlour. She'd arranged her possessions carefully. Each one held a memory of the family or the child who had given it to her.

An old people's home indeed! That's what Edith had suggested for them both. "We'd be properly looked after then, if we're ill or should have a fall," she'd said.

Edith irritated Ada beyond measure with her talk of flats in a community home. She intended to begin a completely new life, to emerge in her own identity as Ada Calthorpe, not just Nanny . . .

For a few short weeks she went to bed when she liked, got up when she felt inclined, ate all the delicious food she'd been denied because it wasn't good for children. Instead of milky puddings and beef tea, she had chilli con carne and spaghetti Bolognese.

Or she could do a bit of weeding in the tiny garden at the back — or she could even pop along to see her neighbour, Luke Endacott.

He was a widower, about Ada's age. Once he'd owned a farm but had sold up when his wife died. For a little while he'd tried living with his married daughter but it hadn't worked. Now he lived in the cottage a few yards up the lane.

He was a quiet sort, like Ada, just in need of some peace and quiet.

But Ada's deserved peace and quiet was shattered that day in early summer when the morning post brought a letter from Edith.

IT was a beautiful morning and sunlight filled the valley. The air was full of the smell of new-mown hay and bruised grass in the sun . . .

The letter said Edith didn't approve of her sister living alone, and she knew her duty as the elder of the two. She was going to sacrifice her own wishes and find a tenant for her beloved flat in the town. She'd move into the cottage, although she hated the country and the sea, but if Ada wouldn't compromise, she had no alternative.

Ada could expect both her luggage and herself next day . . .

"Blast her!" Ada said loudly into the still blue of the day. It was an expression she had picked up from one of her charges who eventually became an admiral.

The next day it looked as though Edith must be moving in for ever. The carrier's van brought two trunks and four suitcases, and later in the day her sister drove up in the ancient village taxi.

Edith had been installed for a week when the trouble started.

Ada had made porridge and covered it with brown sugar and thick dollops of cream. Edith pushed hers away, her eyes were as sharp as her tongue.

"I'm not eating any more of this fattening food, and neither are you," she said, looking at Ada's comfortable but shapeless skirt and cardigan. "You're letting yourself go to seed. Why, you're not even wearing a corset any more!"

Ada offered up a small prayer for patience, and without answering dug her spoon into the thick, delicious, steaming porridge.

Edith sat in stiff disapproval eating her bran and prunes.

So it went on all through the golden days of summer.

Most of all Edith disapproved of Luke.

He was clever with plants and had often given Ada cuttings and seedlings for her garden.

His speciality was dahlias, and already she had a marvellous show.

Edith hated the dahlias with a kind of personal hatred. Whenever she picked them, an earwig invariably fell out. All her life she'd had a horror of what she called creepy-crawlies.

In the past Luke had sometimes shared Ada's evening meal. But Edith soon put a stop to that by making it so obvious she disapproved, that the poor man had shrivelled up and gone back into the shell from which Ada had patiently managed to coax him.

Daily the tension increased. Often Ada would sneak out of the back door while Edith sat with her never-ending knitting, and take Luke a bowl of hot food for his evening meal.

"There's talk in the village," Edith said one morning. She cracked her breakfast egg with a certain amount of violence, as if it were Ada's guilty head.

"Oh?" Ada cared little for what the village thought.

" 'Bout you and that Luke Endacott." Edith paused, her silence heavy with meaning and implied criticism.

Ada laughed. "They've no call, we're hardly in our first flush!"

From then on things went from bad to worse. Edith adopted a martyred air as she had when they were children and Ada was guilty of some misdemeanour. It grated on Ada now as it had then.

She hadn't asked her sister to come, she argued with herself, but a little voice inside told her she should appreciate her sister's concern. She supposed she did, deep down, but she'd been so used to a certain amount of personal independence, even though she'd worked for someone else.

Still, she could understand Edith thinking of her cosy flat back in town, with all her own furniture and possessions, now being lived in by strangers. Edith was deeply involved in the Townswomen's Guild, too, and there was nothing here to match that.

All this Ada had gathered from the hints that Edith had dropped. Granted, they might not be her own cup of tea, but they were her sister's. In a way she must feel lonely here . . .

The Wonder Of A Water Garden

Adding the luxury of a pond in your garden isn't as difficult as you might think. All it takes is a little time and patience — and our easy guidelines.

THERE is magic in a pool, for even a small one brings life and movement to a garden. You don't even have to construct one yourself these days, unless you're really keen on do-it-yourself. Nowadays, you can buy a pool ready made in Fibreglass and just sink it in the chosen place.

But, having got everything prepared, a sparkling pool with plants and fish doesn't happen overnight. You have to strike a balance between plant and animal life.

The main obstacle is algae, a minute form of plant life, that spreads and multiplies in sunlight, making the water discoloured. If you plant water lilies and the white-flowered "Water Soldier" (Stratiotes), the shade from thin floating leaves restricts the growth of algae, but until these plants become established, the algae will continue to flourish.

So the next thing needed is underwater plants, known as oxygenators. These help to clear the water and provide food and shelter for fish later on. One of the best is Elodea Canadensis, sometimes referred to as Anacharis. It is a rapid grower with dark green spiky foliage.

Hottonia Palustris, the Water Violet, is useful too and holds its mauve flowers above the water while the pretty fern-like leaves are submerged. The light green Callitriche, "Starwort," is another good one. Then some water fleas (Daphnia) are necessary as well. They will feed on the algae and in turn be eaten by the fish.

Ada sighed. She couldn't think of a ready solution. One which would suit them both and damage neither, salve Edith's conscience, and yet still let her feel she'd done her bit.

As it happened Ada was quite right in her idea. Now the summer was fading into autumn Edith had begun to long for the warmth and comfort of her own little home. She missed the central heating, the lights in the shops, the cheerful company of old friends.